JAPANESE MYTHS

JAPANESE MYTHS

HEROES, GODS, DEMONS AND LEGENDS

MELANIE CLEGG

amber
BOOKS

First published in 2023

Published by
Amber Books Ltd
United House
North Road
London N7 9DP
United Kingdom
www.amberbooks.co.uk
Instagram: amberbooksltd
Facebook: amberbooks
Pinterest: amberbooksltd

Editor: Michael Spilling
Designer: Jeremy Williams
Picture researcher: Terry Forshaw

ISBN: 978-1-83886-318-0

Printed in China

CONTENTS

INTRODUCTION

For as long as there have been people, there have been myths. Myths are, put simply, stories and narratives that express a culture's understanding of itself and its reality. They are central to cultural identity and can be used to support, explain or justify the structures of that society. Myths express what makes a culture unique, as well as concepts that are universal to humanity.

Definitions of what represents a 'myth' versus a 'legend' are hazy; myth is often understood to be a type of symbolic storytelling, whereas legends are rooted in historical events and figures. Still, these categories are nebulous and the crossover so great that the terms are frequently used interchangeably, at least outside of academic writing. And, we will see as we begin to look at Japanese myths, legends and folklore, that when looking back to the distant past it can be difficult to distinguish 'truth' and historical fact from fiction. For example, creation myths have at various times been regarded as both historical truth and

OPPOSITE: **A warrior slays a giant white ape in this woodblock print by artist Yoshitora Utagawa.**

fictional metaphor. Ultimately, whether they are 'true' or not is not what matters; they remain important for the way they became inextricably entwined with Japanese culture and society.

In *The Oxford Companion to World Mythology* the US academic David Leeming describes myths as 'cultural and universal human dreams' and summarizes them succinctly:

'Surely both definitions of myths, as illusory stories and as containers of eternal truth, are valid simultaneously. The sacred products of the human imagination are in some sense true in ways that history cannot be. Myths might be considered the most basic expressions of a defining aspect of the human species – the need and ability to understand and to tell stories to reflect our understanding, whether or not we know the real facts. Humans, unlike other animals, are blessed or cursed with consciousness and specifically with the consciousness of plot – of beginnings, middles, and ends. We wonder individually, culturally, and as a species about our origins and about the significance of our present time, and we think continually of the future. We are always aware of the journey aspect of our existence. So it has always been that adults have told stories to children to describe our journey, and leaders have told their people stories for the same reason.'

Under the umbrella term 'Japanese mythology' there exists a host of narratives from oral folk traditions to written accounts commissioned by the ruling elite, from Shinto tales to Buddhist parables, from stories of native origin to those imported from China and India. The roots of some are shrouded in mystery, whereas others can be traced back to specific points in history; most can offer us some insight into the societal norms, cultural mores and artistic tastes of the time.

BELOW: **The Buddha is flanked by a pair of bodhisattvas in this carved tile from the Asuka period.**

Japanese History

Japan's history is generally divided into eras that broadly align with the power structures of each timeframe. This also allows us to track cultural changes and identify broad trends in art, literature and society. The first written texts appeared in the 8th century, but knowledge of early history can be gleaned from archaeological remains and artifacts as well as Chinese and Korean records of the period.

Japanese history as understood today is, broadly speaking, one of fragmented groups consolidating political power for a time before breaking apart again and repeating the cycle. As each dominating group rose to power, myth and its corresponding ritual was often used as a sociopolitical tool of the elite to justify and lend authority to their rule.

Much of what is today referred to as 'Japanese mythology' can be traced back to two texts written in the 8th century: the *Kojiki* and the *Nihon Shoki*. These compiled the nation's native myths and historical accounts, which at the time were considered analogous.

The *Kojiki*

The *Kojiki*, or *Record of Ancient Matters*, is the oldest written work in Japan, compiled in 712 after a writing system was introduced from China in the 6th century. It is a chronicle of myths, legends,

ABOVE: **This folding screen features a scene of the Battle of Yashima from *The Tale of the Heike*, an epic account of the Genpei War.**

HISTORICAL TIMELINE

Jomon period (10,000–300BCE)
The prehistoric period is named for the distinctive rope pattern designs found on pottery from this era. The first settled communities emerge and primitive agriculture appears, although the population are mostly hunter-gatherers. According to myth, this is when the land of Japan was founded by Emperor Jimmu.

Yayoi period (300BCE–250CE)
The Yayoi period sees new forms of pottery together with advancements in architecture and carpentry, and the start of intensive rice agriculture in paddy fields.

Kofun period (250–538)
In this period of protohistory characterized by kofun monumental tombs, political power starts to be centralized in the south-western plains. The earliest written histories date their records to around this time.

Asuka period (538–710)
Buddhism is introduced via China along with writing, architecture and Chinese art styles. Japan starts to model itself on Chinese civilization. Powerful clan rulers emerge, among them the Yamato who founded the imperial dynasty that will last until the present day.

Nara (710–794)
The first permanent capital is established at Nara. Society is predominantly agricultural and centres around village life where people follow traditional Shinto religion. The elite adopt Chinese fashions, their writing system, and Buddhism.

Heian period (794–1192)
Culture flourishes in the new capital at Heian-kyo (present-day Kyoto). The court models itself on the Chinese monarchy. A unique phonetic script develops and the imperial court refines its art and literature, with court women playing an active part. An aristocratic elite starts to accumulate wealth and trade systems emerge. The monk Kūkai introduces esoteric Shingon Buddhism to Japan.

Kamakura period (1192–1333)
The imperial court loses its grip on power as the Minamoto and Taira warrior clans clash during the Genpei War. Minamoto no Yoritomo emerges victorious and establishes the first feudal government, called the shogunate. The capital is moved to Kamakura where many temples are built, and a warrior class of samurai develops. Zen Buddhism is introduced.

Muromachi period (1338–1477)
Power moves back to Kyoto and feudalism is fully established. Samurai and court culture merges and the arts, such as the tea ceremony, Noh theatre and ink wash painting, flourish.

Sengoku period (1477–1573)
Also known as the Warring States period, it is a time of civil war and social

upheaval. Central power dissipates and local warlords, called daimyo, gain power and construct great castles surrounded by feudal towns.

Azuchi-Momoyama period (1573–1603)
Powerful warlords begin the process of reunifying the country. Three key unifiers emerge: Oda Nobunaga, Toyotomi Hideyoshi and Tokugawa Ieyasu.

Edo period (1603–1868)
The country is unified under the rule of a military government known as the shogunate or bakufu, creating a period of peace and stability. Power is concentrated in the capital of Edo (modern-day Tokyo) where a distinct urban culture develops along with a wealthy merchant class. Printing technology proliferates art and literature. The country is closed to foreign access in a policy called sakoku.

Bakumatsu period (1853–68)
A brief period in which the Tokugawa bakufu government is overthrown. Captain Perry's Black Ships arrive from America at the small fishing port of Yokohama and Japan is forced to open its borders to the world. Beginning of modernization and industrialization.

Meiji period (1868–1912)
Power is restored to the emperor and a modern nation state takes form. New science and technology bring modern inventions, and the influx of new ideas from Western nations has a profound effect on Japan's social, political and economic structures. Japan claims military victories over China and Russia and annexes Korea and Taiwan.

Taisho period (1912–26)
A time of great flux as a liberal movement, Taishō Democracy, begins. World War I brings economic prosperity as Japan manufactures war materiel for Europe. Towards the end of the era, social unrest including rice riots and acts of political terrorism result in a shift in power back to pro-military leaders.

Early Shōwa period (1926–45)
Growing nationalism and militarization combined with Japan's imperial ambitions in East Asia eventually lead to the Pacific War and the country's subsequent defeat by the Allied Forces after the atomic bombings of Hiroshima and Nagasaki.

Late Shōwa period (1945–89)
Also referred to as the post-war period. Japan gradually recovers from World War II and experiences an unprecedented era of growth referred to as the 'economic miracle'.

Heisei period (1989–2019)
Japan flexes its soft power and cultural exports such as anime, manga and Japanese food increase as inbound tourism also grows.

Reiwa period (2019–present)
With the abdication of Emperor Akihito, his son Naruhito ascends to the throne, and the period is named Reiwa.

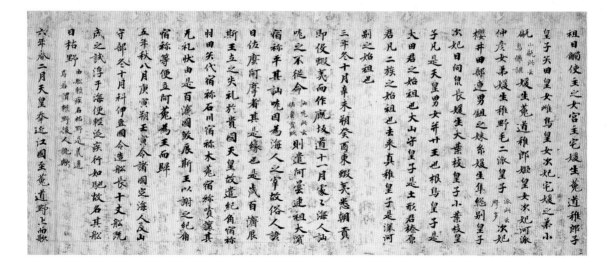

ABOVE: A page from the
Tanaka version of the
Nihon Shoki, one of
Japan's oldest written
works.

folklore, genealogy and historical accounts that record the
origins of Japan, its gods and the imperial line. As with many
origin mythologies, it is a blend of the fantastical together with
references to real-life events and people.

The archaic language makes it a difficult text to translate into
English, but the immense work has been undertaken several
times. The first was by Basil Hall Chamberlain in 1882. Most
recently, Gustav Heldt published his updated translation in 2014.

The *Nihon Shoki*

The *Nihon Shoki,* or *Chronicles of Japan,* is the second-oldest
written work and covers largely the same content as the *Kojiki.*
It is, however, longer and more detailed, and while the *Kojiki*
contains only one version of events, the *Nihon Shoki* sometimes
records one or more alternate accounts.

The text is attributed to Ō no Yasumaro, an aristocrat who
was commissioned to write it by Empress Genshō in 711 under the
editorial supervision of Prince Toneri. The first English-language
translation was completed by William George Aston in 1896.

Shinto

After the introduction of Buddhism to Japan, it became necessary
to distinguish it from the pre-existing native folk religion, which
subsequently became known as Shinto. The belief system is
polytheistic and animistic. It is based around local deities or

spirits known as *kami* and their associated rituals, as well as veneration of the dead. *Kami* reside not only in major natural features such as the sun and mountains, but in trees, springs, rocks and other natural features. Many are tutelary deities, acting as guardians of particular places, people or concepts.

Such folk beliefs belonged to a local, oral tradition until a selection were compiled in the *Kojiki* and *Nihon Shoki*, thus joining these disparate traditions into a constructed mythos that could be defined as the mainy Japanese canon. Rituals became codified and worship of the major deities spread nationwide. Still, minor local myths and traditions remained, their *kami* coexisting peacefully with the national figureheads. Many of the Shinto religious rituals, which include purification, prayer and offerings to the *kami*, as well as more elaborate festivals and celebrations, are still observed today not only by dedicated priests, but as cultural practices by ordinary Japanese people.

BELOW: **A sculpture of a Shinto deity dating from the Heian period.**

Buddhism

Buddhism is a vast and complex network of thought and religious practices that can be traced back to ancient India in the 5th century BC. After spreading to Korea and China, its beliefs were later transmitted to Japan from around the 6th century. During this time, Buddhism was adopted as the official court religion in the capital of Nara and later Heian-kyo (present-day Kyoto). Different sects and types of Buddhism continued to find their way to Japan over the centuries, often from China, the major ones being Tendai, Shingon and eventually Zen and Nichiren. While the many sects of

Buddhism that have existed and continue to exist in Japan differ greatly in their beliefs, rituals and deities, they have all drawn on the same vast pool of mythology.

Shinbutsu-shūgō

This is a key concept in Japanese mythology and religion that literally means 'fusion of kami and buddhas', and refers to the syncretism of Shinto and Buddhism. Syncretism is the practice of combining different belief systems through the merging or assimilation of traditions that were once distinct from one another. This can create an overarching cultural unity as well as allow for the inclusion rather than rejection of different faiths and schools of thought.

By the time Buddhism was introduced to Japan during the Asuka period (538–710), there was already a thriving, but disparate, native Shinto belief system with which it had to be reconciled. To do this, Buddhist temples were often attached to

BELOW: **Fushimi Inari Shrine in Kyoto, famous for its red** *torii* **gates, is the head shrine for the Shinto** *kami* **Inari.**

local Shinto shrines, and could be devoted to both *kami* and buddha at the same time, essentially conflating the two.

Buddhism already had a long history of syncretization via its journey through India, China and Korea, and monks in Japan were ready to seek the origins of their native *kami* in the Buddhist scriptures. At first, *kami* were often treated like any other being who was in need of salvation via Buddhism. Later, with the declaration of the *kami* Hachiman to be a bodhisattva, it became the norm for *kami* to be closely associated with Buddhist deities. This led to the development of *honji-suijaku*, a theory that explained how native *kami* were emanations of buddhas, meaning they could be worshipped within Buddhism. The way in which *kami* were integrated into the Buddhist canon depended on the sect, but the entanglement of Shinto and Buddhism became so complete that even after a government-mandated separation order it was impossible to sever them.

Shinbutsu-bunri

After the Restoration of 1868, the newly founded Meiji government sought to reverse the amalgamation that had taken place over the past centuries with a separation order that called for the 'separation of kami and buddhas'. At a time of rapid modernization and Western influence, many conservatives wanted to protect what they saw as 'Japanese values', and Shinto was seen as a pure native belief system whereas Buddhism was a foreign importation. There was also a practical reason; Buddhist sects had amassed great wealth and power that could potentially threaten the new government.

The governmental intellectual elite worked to promote a cohesive *kokutai*, or national polity, that would unite the Japanese people around the divine figure of the emperor. Shinto beliefs supported the idea of the emperor's lineage reaching back to the sun goddess Amaterasu, and as such was an important tool for elevating the emperor to divine status and legitimizing his rule.

Although the policy was ultimately unsuccessful, it defined Shinto and Buddhism as distinct religions in the public consciousness, even if the lines between them remain blurred and many people participate in practices from both.

KAMI WERE OFTEN TREATED LIKE ANY OTHER BEING WHO WAS IN NEED OF SALVATION VIA BUDDHISM.

ABOVE: **This print by Kunitoshi Baiju (1847–1899) depicts the issuance of the Meiji constitution.**

The Modern Nation State

What is now termed 'state Shinto' became a vehicle for rising nationalism as Japan's leaders built a modern nation state on the back of its mythology. The Meiji Restoration of 1868 put the emperor back in power, with the new Meiji Constitution declaring him to be 'sacred and inviolable', and asserted his divine right to rule based on his direct lineage from the sun goddess Amaterasu as recorded in the *Kojiki*.

There was a concerted ideological effort to 'renovate' Japanese society, and the two chronicles played an important part, their myths being disseminated in classrooms across Japan as historical fact. Native legends and folk tales that were considered to promote Japanese values were used for children's reading practice, and historical figures such as the Forty-seven *Rōnin* became propaganda aimed at encouraging absolute loyalty to the nation. *Kokugaku*, the 'national study' of ancient Japanese literature and culture, grew as an academic sphere and scholars played an active part in asserting the superiority of the *kokutai* or national polity. At the same time, minority ethnic groups were actively oppressed and assimilated into the empire in an effort to establish the concept of the homogeneity of the Japanese people.

Later, after Japan's defeat in World War II, Emperor Hirohito renounced his claim to divinity under the influence of the occupying US forces. A new Constitution of Japan was promulgated, formally renouncing war and putting sovereignty in the hands of the people and rendering the emperor a figurehead who served as 'the symbol of the State and of the unity of the people'. Suddenly, the creation myths were once more simply stories; although their enduring influence remained a part of the fabric of Japanese culture.

The Ainu

The Ainu are the indigenous people of northern Japan in areas today known as Hokkaido, Sakhalin and the Kurils. They were subjugated and assimilated into the nation of Japan in the late 1800s after the imperial government's annexation of Hokkaido. The Ainu have a language and culture distinct from the Japanese, although their numbers today are small. In 2019, the Japanese

BELOW: **Ainu women perform a crane dance.**

government finally acknowledged them as an ethnically distinct group, although ethnic homogeneity remains a cornerstone of Japanese national identity.

The Ainu people were primarily hunter-gatherers as well as seafarers. They lived in relatively isolated groups, which contributed to a disparate mythology where stories and events were assigned to different deities depending on the local tradition. With no indigenous writing system, Ainu mythology was passed down orally in the form of epic verses called *kamuy yukar*, which were memorized and recited at communal gatherings. Ainu deities are called *kamuy* and we will discuss these further in later chapters. Another Ainu belief is in the idea of *ramat*, a power found in all living things as well as inanimate objects that is similar to the Polynesian concept of mana. It inhabits anything that is whole and working but leaves it upon the death of the living thing or destruction of the object.

The Ryukyuans

The Ryukyu Islands – stretching between the southern coast of Japan and the northern coast of Taiwan and including the island of Okinawa – were an independent kingdom up to the 17th century, when they were conquered by the Satsuma clan of Japan. Today, despite being a distinct ethnolinguistic group, Ryukyuans are not officially recognized by the Japanese government as a minority group, and have been considered 'Japanese' since the annexation and assimilation campaign by the Empire of Japan in the late 19th century. Nonetheless, there are around 1.4 million people in Okinawa Prefecture who identify as Ryukyuan and who maintain their distinct culture, although the Ryukyuan languages are in danger of dying out.

Ryukyuan and Okinawan culture and religion were influenced by China and Japan, as the kingdom conducted trade with both. The first official history of the Ryukyu Kingdom was compiled in 1650 by Shō Shōken and is called the *Chūzan Seikan*. It features creation myths about the kingdom's founding, however, the work is generally regarded as a constructed narrative inspired by political interests, and was used by the Meiji government to legitimize Japan's claim to the area. In general, Ryukyuan myths and deities tend to be vague and undefined. Many of the myths that were once considered native to the Ryukyu Islands have since been reexamined as interpretations made through the lens of mainland Japanese scholars. The lack of primary contemporaneous written sources makes it difficult to distinguish between truly indigenous tales and mythology that has been assigned after the fact.

Although the deities and myths may be amorphous, ritual holds an important place within Ryukyuan culture and daily life. The indigenous religion is female-centric, with most priests and mediums being female, and it focuses on ancestor worship, household gods, protective spirits and sacred places.

Nihonjinron

After the post-war renunciation of war and the emperor's declaration that he was not a direct descendant of the sun goddess, there was a distinct void that had once been filled by Japan's mythology and its divine origins. Influenced by the *kokugaku* of the Edo period, works discussing Japanese national and cultural identity surged in popularity in what can be seen as a response to the country's crushing defeat in World War II and an attempt to assert Japan's place in the new world order.

The genre was named *nihonjinron*, or 'theories of the Japanese people', and common themes included the idea that the Japanese race is unique and that

BELOW: **A photo of Shō Tai (1843–1901), the last king of the kingdom of Ryukyu.**

Japanese culture developed in isolation on their island nation without external influence. It asserts that the Japanese language, too, is unique, leading to a unique psychology and society, and that the very geography and climate of Japan is singular, with Japan being the only country with four seasons. In English-language study, *nihonjinron* is often referred to as 'the myth of Japanese uniqueness'. It is a way of thinking that persists to this day, with many Japanese people accepting such assertions as fact.

Nihonjinron has been used to portray aspects of Japanese culture in both a positive and a negative light. For example, in the immediate post-war period, it served as an attempt to identify what was holding Japan back as it sought to re-establish itself on the world stage, whereas during the 1970s economic boom, it was used to explain Japan's successes as being intrinsically linked to the 'Japanese way' of doing things.

Weird and Wonderful Variety

In addition to the overarching mythology that was codified in the official chronicles written by the ruling elite are a seemingly infinite collection of ghosts and goblins, folk tales and didactic teachings, legends and local lore. Some are specific to very small

BELOW: **Japanese dignitaries arrive to participate in the ceremony of surrender aboard the USS *Missouri* in Tokyo Bay on September 2, 1945.**

local areas, whereas others have been told around the country with regional variations.

The most enduring stories succeed in combining moral lessons about bravery, loyalty or piety with entertainment value. Folk heroes such as Issun-bōshi and Momotaro are beloved for their fantastical origins and enthralling adventures. The stories of Kaguya-hime the Moon Maiden and Urashima Tarō can be considered proto-science fiction with their creative plots that involve travel through space and time. Comedy, too, plays a part in many myths, legends and folklore; even in the *Kojiki* and *Nihon Shoki* we find bawdy and humorous tales, including how the sun goddess Amaterasu was essentially lured out of her cave by a striptease performance.

Another fascinating aspect of Japanese folklore is the menagerie of strange creatures known as *yōkai*. They range from the terrifying to the comedic and absurd; the *tanuki* is known for its comically large testicles that can be thrown over

ABOVE: **Cosplayers wear costumes inspired by spirits and creatures from Japanese folklore.**

JAPAN IN TRANSLATION

The study of Japan and Japanese texts in English would be impossible without the work of scholars, linguistic experts and translators. After Japan opened its borders in the late 19th century, foreign diplomats and scholars took up posts there and started to produce writings and research in European languages. Books on Japan and collections of stories became popular overseas, as did Japanese art and aesthetics – the craze was called *Japonisme* by the French. Many of these late 19th- and early 20th-century texts are valuable resources for Japanologists today, but it is important to acknowledge that they sit firmly within the time period in which they were written and also to bear in mind that, while translations may serve as primary sources, they are one step removed from the original source material and will inevitably contain the interpretations and biases of the translator. In a few cases, what was presented as a native Japanese story was in fact merely inspired by local tales and mostly rewritten to appeal to an overseas audience.

Below are some of the English-language scholars of culture, history, language, religion and mythology that have shaped Western studies of Japan.

Lafcadio Hearn (1850–1904)
The most famous of early Western scholars of Japan, Hearn's writings, particularly his collections of ghost stories, opened Japan up to readers around the world. He was also a popular figure within Japan, where he remains fondly remembered.

Algernon Bertram Mitford (1837–1916)
A British diplomat who popularized Japanese legends in his book *Tales of Old Japan* (1871), which introduced *The Forty-seven Rōnin* to English-speaking audiences.

William George Aston (1841–1911)
Originally from Ireland, Aston served as a diplomat and was one of the founders of modern Japanese studies. He was the first person to translate the *Nihon Shoki* into English.

Sir Ernest Mason Satow (1843–1929)
Known as Ainosuke Satō in Japan, Satow was a founding member of the Asiatic Society of Japan in 1872. A talented linguist, he worked as a British diplomat in several Asian countries and was particularly influential in Anglo-Japanese relations.

Yei Theodora Ozaki (1870–1932)
The daughter of a Japanese father and English mother, Ozaki's translations of Japanese folk tales into English fairy tales for children popularized tales such as *Peach Boy* in the West.

Basil Hall Chamberlain (1850–1935)
A British academic and a professor of the Japanese language at Tokyo Imperial University, Chamberlain wrote extensively on Japanese literature and was the first person to translate the *Kojiki* into

English. He also studied the Ainu and the Ryukyuan languages.

Takejirō Hasegawa (1853–1938)

Hasegawa employed foreign translators and writers in Japan and published Japan-related books in European languages. His series of Japanese folk tales was a huge hit with foreign residents in Japan and with overseas audiences.

Florence Sakade (1916–1999)

Born in Japan, Sakade lived abroad during her childhood before returning to Tokyo to work at the Charles E. Tuttle Company where she served as an editor on hundreds of English-language books related to Japan. Her 1958 *Japanese Children's Favorite Stories* introduced Japanese fairy tales to a generation of young readers.

Haruo Shirane (1951–present)

Professor of Japanese Literature and Culture at Columbia University in New York, Shirane has consistently published on medieval Japanese literature and has been particularly influential in the field of classical Japanese linguistics.

A photograph of Yukio Ozaki and his wife Yei Theodora Ozaki. Ozaki is considered the father of the modern Japanese constitution.

its shoulder. Meanwhile ghosts, or *yūrei*, feature in gruesome and blood-curdling tales that have become the foundation of modern Japanese horror.

The vast canon of Japanese stories and creatures have been passed on originally through oral storytelling, then by printed written and illustrated works, and in more recent times via new forms of mass media and the internet. Japanese children today grow up with many of the same tales as their counterparts in the distant past thanks to new retellings that refresh the old classics, and each generation brings its own take on the familiar myths, allowing people to continue to enjoy them through an evolving sociological landscape.

Myth in Everyday Life

Although myth and folklore are kept alive in literature, entertainment, culture and modes of thought, they also remain embedded in everyday tradition and superstition. This includes small, personal actions such as lighting an incense offering for departed family members at the household shrine, as well as large-scale traditional celebrations. The festivals that take place throughout the calendar year have their roots in ancient religion and folklore, and are times when people come together as families or communities to share traditional dance, music, food and drink. Many customs have become more secular than religious; for example, it is common for Japanese people to take part in *hatsumode* – the first shrine or temple visit of the new year – even if they do not identify as Shinto or Buddhist practitioners. People attend either a shrine or temple to make their wishes for the new year and purchase *omikuji* fortunes and *omamori* protective charms, and there is no expectation that attendees be devout believers. In fact, many people visit shrines out of superstition and tradition rather than formal religious faith, for example, students going to pray before exams in the hope that it will help them pass. There is a generally held notion within Japanese society that religious and spiritual beliefs and practices form part of the culture as a whole, and that the beliefs of different religions need not be exclusive from one another, nor incompatible with an overall secular life.

THE FESTIVALS THAT TAKE PLACE THROUGHOUT THE CALENDAR YEAR HAVE THEIR ROOTS IN ANCIENT RELIGION AND FOLKLORE, AND ARE TIMES WHEN PEOPLE COME TOGETHER AS FAMILIES OR COMMUNITIES.

Folklore and Netlore

In the modern era, advances in technology have corresponded with the proliferation of new forms of art and literature. For example, new printing methods in the Edo period allowed for written works to be produced and distributed faster and more easily than before. This led to printed materials becoming accessible to the lower classes and so spurred demand for different types of stories and images.

Similarly, in the 21st century the internet has facilitated the creation and dissemination of new urban legends and 'netlore', a kind of folklore that is circulated via the World Wide Web. Just as villagers centuries ago participated in the creation of their own local, miniature mythologies, today netizens have formed online communities with their own traditions and lore. Sometimes, these become so popular that they spread across social platforms and make the jump to mainstream media, eventually becoming part of the popular consciousness.

ABOVE: People line up to do *hatsumode*, the first shrine visit of the new year, outside Nishinomiya Shrine in Hyōgo prefecture.

Pop Culture

Popular culture including mass media, such as films, anime, manga comics and video games, is enjoyed by the general population as entertainment while also having an influence on society and attitudes. Just as we see ancient Norse gods gracing our screen in the Marvel Cinematic Universe films, many figures from native myth and legend are also mainstays of Japanese pop culture. Franchises such as *Pokémon* and *Yo-Kai Watch* took inspiration from the *yōkai* encyclopedias and card games of the Edo period to make creature collectathons that have become global hits. And in recent years, Japanese mythology has been mined for characters to feature in *gacha* games, video games primarily released on mobile platforms that feature collectible characters or items that users are encouraged to spend money on acquiring through gambling mechanics. A short-lived mobile game, *Namu Amida Butsu! Rendai Utena*, even reimagined Buddhist gods as handsome anime men for the player to collect and battle with. Similarly, *Ayakashi Rumble* features a dizzying array of deities, *yōkai*, historical figures and fictional characters portrayed as cute anime girls, often skimpily dressed in costumes inspired by traditional Japanese garments. In another example of the harmonious blending of religious belief and everyday culture, there is no public outcry over these depictions, even when they portray deities that are still worshipped by millions of Shinto or Buddhist believers.

Many products have used their 'Japaneseness' as a selling point to find global success. For example, the 2006 action-adventure video game *Ōkami* is set in the classical world of myth and legend and has a distinctive art style steeped in Japanese mythology and aesthetics. It was released in English to critical acclaim in 2008. The 2016 film *Kimi no na wa*, released in English as *Your Name*, draws on Shinto and associated imagery to tell a romantic story with fantasy elements that won multiple awards. The aesthetics and imagery of Japanese mythology and folklore have proved appealing to international audiences and are used as a form of soft power by the Japanese government to market Japan to the world as 'Cool Japan', thus boosting the nation's cultural capital on the global stage and further promoting the 'myth' of Japanese uniqueness.

Japanese culture, history, art and mythology are unique in the way that all cultures are unique. While we can find aspects that are distinct and peculiar to a particular culture, at the same time we can also encounter commonalities that speak to a shared and universal human experience.

BELOW: *Your Name*, a 2016 animated film by Makoto Shinkai, is firmly rooted in Japanese culture and proved to be a hit with international audiences.

꿈 속에서 시작된 기적 같은 사랑 이야기

너의이름은.
your name.

아직 만난 적 없는 너를,
찾고 있어

신카이 마코토 감독 작품

2017. 1.4 WWW.YOUR-NAME.KR

A note on the text

The stories told here are – in the mythic tradition – retellings based upon retellings based upon yet more retellings, and as such should not be taken as gospel. They are sourced from a combination of English- and Japanese-language sources, and have been rewritten to suit the format of this book.

1

CREATION MYTHS AND COSMOLOGY

Although myths and legends provide entertainment, they can also serve as a lens through which to understand culture. The mythology of a specific culture and how people interact with this mythos can both provide insight into that culture and have lasting effects on it. In particular, creation myths are a way for a people to explain who they are and why they are here.

Although these myths are generally no longer accepted as historical fact, their influence on a nation's understanding of itself endures.

However, before we jump into these fantastical, fanciful and at times messy (bodily fluids are a common feature) stories, let us first consider a few things to keep in mind.

Texts: contents and purpose
Although the *Kojiki* and the *Nihon Shoki* represent the oldest written accounts of Japanese myths, there was undoubtedly a rich

OPPOSITE: **Uzume no Mikoto dances to lure the sun goddess Amaterasu out of her cave in this print by Totoya Hokkei (1780–1850) from his series 'The Spring Cave'.**

oral tradition that preceded them. It is important to remember that the stories in these chronicles are the ones that were chosen to be recorded, and that they were likely told in a specific way and for a particular reason. The works have a noticeable preoccupation with lineage, with many heavenly family trees being traced directly to earthly descendants in families that existed in the imperial court of the time. It is widely understood in modern scholarship that these books were compiled not simply as a record of mythology, but to justify the rule of the imperial and aristocratic families by tying them directly to the deities and to the sun goddess Amaterasu.

The contents of these ancient texts will have been understood in different ways and have had different meanings to people at various times throughout the centuries. When these texts were first compiled, we can assume that they were treated as an official history, and that people believed in them as historical fact. Now, the earlier parts of the texts and the figures who appear within them are regarded as completely mythical, however, some of the later parts of each volume that relate to the imperial court have been corroborated with contemporary Chinese and Korean documents. Modern scholars read the *Kojiki* and the *Nihon*

BELOW: *Kokugaku* scholar Motoori Norinaga spent 34 years studying the *Kojiki* and composing his 44-volume *Commentary on the Kojiki,* now housed in the Honori Norinaga Memorial Museum.

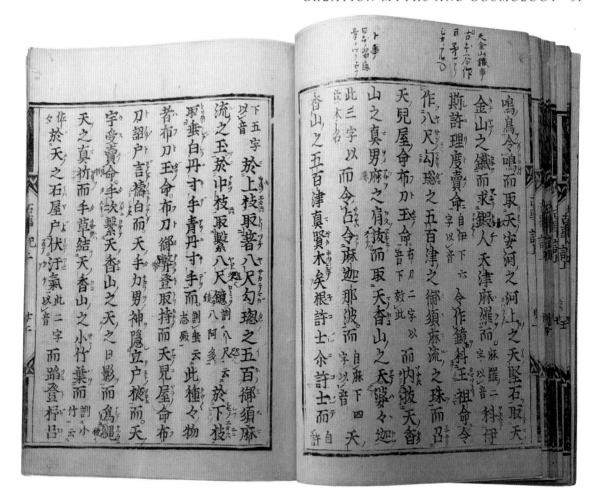

Shoki as allegory while looking to the texts for insight into early Japanese life and thought. Like other defining texts such as the Bible or the *Iliad*, their contents have been interpreted, debated and reinterpreted across the centuries.

Genealogy and naming conventions

As with any pantheon, as we go down the generations of gods the complexity of their family trees increases almost exponentially, with many gods and goddesses giving birth to a seemingly infinite array of both named and unnamed deities.

An added complexity is that of Japanese naming conventions, particularly in ancient times. Many *kami* have multiple names that are used interchangeably or go through a sequence of name changes corresponding with changes to their status. This applies not only to the mythical but to the mundane, with many real

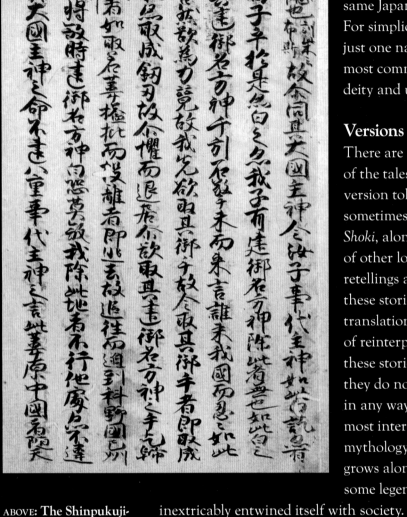

ABOVE: **The Shinpukuji-bon manuscript (1371–1372) is the oldest existing manuscript of the Kojiki.**

historical figures also going by several names. In addition, there are different ways of rendering the same Japanese name into English. For simplicity's sake, we will pick just one name – usually the one most commonly used – for each deity and use this consistently.

Versions

There are many different versions of the tales told below, with one version told in the *Kojiki* and sometimes several in the *Nihon Shoki*, along with an assortment of other local variations, retellings and so on. Discussing these stories in their English translations adds yet another layer of reinterpretation. In reading these stories, keep in mind that they do not claim to be definitive in any way; in fact, one of the most interesting things about mythology is the way it lives and grows alongside humanity, like some legendary creature that has inextricably entwined itself with society.

Gods of Creation

As with so many creation myths, in the beginning, there was chaos.

The original *kami*

Then, the original *kami* popped into being out of nothingness. The accounts are vague and conflicting in terms of their number, but it seems that the first deity, who is referred to by different names in the *Kojiki* and the *Nihon Shoki*, was soon followed by several more, all also genderless and shapeless. These deities are often referred to as the amatsukami or heavenly deities. The only original deity who features much in later stories is Takamimusubi, the grandfather of Ninigi, who we will meet later.

The divine generations

Not much is known about the original deities or their descendants, many of whom appear only as names in the chronicles. After these first single deities came seven more generations of deities, some of whom appeared alone and some as a pair. These are the Seven Divine Generations. The last of the seventh generation were a male and female pair who would become the primal couple.

The primal couple: Izanagi and Izanami

At this point, the land was a formless, unconsolidated substance. Now, the other deities commanded the last two, whose names

ONE OF THE MOST INTERESTING THINGS ABOUT MYTHOLOGY IS THE WAY IT LIVES AND GROWS ALONGSIDE HUMANITY, LIKE SOME LEGENDARY CREATURE.

AINU CREATION MYTHS

There are many different Ainu creation myths, some of which share similarities with those of Japan. Here is one such story.

In the beginning there was only a sludge of water and earth. In the clouds were thunder demons and the first *kamuy* who came from nothing. These *kamuy* sent down a bird spirit in the form of a water wagtail. The little wagtail flitted over the swamp,

pounding here and there with its feet and tail. As it stomped the sludge down, areas of dry land formed like patches floating in the surrounding water.

Now the first *kamuy* sent down other *kamuy*, such as the fire spirit, hunting spirit and water spirit. The fire spirit would come to be worshipped as the most important deity, the goddess of the hearth, and would serve as a connection between humans and the *kamuy*, sending their prayers and offerings to the right places.

ABOVE: **Izanagi and Izanami as depicted by woodblock print artist Sukenobu Nishikawa (1671–1750).**

OPPOSITE: **Izanami and Izanagi consolidating the land with the heavenly jewelled spear 'Ama-no-Nuboko' by painter and printmaker Eitaku Kobayashi (1843–1890).**

were Izanagi and Izanami, to solidify the land. They granted to the pair a heavenly bejewelled spear, and the two stood upon the Floating Bridge of Heaven and used the spear to stir the formless mass. When the mass became thick and curdled, they withdrew the spear; as they did so, droplets fell from the tip to form a solid island, which was called Onogoro.

The heavenly pair descended from Heaven to the Island of Onogoro. Here, they built a heavenly pillar and a palace. Soon, they noted the similarities and differences in their bodies, and Izanagi suggested, in wonderfully euphemistic terms, that he insert his 'excess' into Izanami's 'insufficiency'. Izanami agreed, and so the two set out to walk around the pillar, he from the left and she from the right, to meet for conjugal intercourse. This they did, and upon meeting around the pillar, Izanami exclaimed in delight at seeing her spouse.

After getting on with the business of procreation, Izanami gave birth to Hiruko the Leech Child, a deformed creature devoid of limbs. This did not seem right to them, so they placed the baby in a reed boat and let it float away. The couple then birthed an island made of froth and foam, which also did not count among their children. Following this, they ascended to Heaven to seek counsel from the senior deities as to why their children were not good; the Heavenly Deities responded that it was because Izanami, the woman, had spoken first upon rounding the pillar. They recommended the couple descend and try again. Izanagi and Izanami walked around the pillar once again, and when they met this time, Izanagi was the first to speak, delighting at his wife before she responded in kind.

Birth of the islands

After performing the ritual correctly, the couple gave birth to healthy and good children who formed the islands that would make up Japan. The order of creation of the islands differs depending on the narrative, with Shikoku and Kyushu usually being among the firstborn. Following this, Izanami also birthed various features of the natural world such as mountains, seas, rivers, forests and plains. These children, representing the natural features, were also deities, in male–female pairs.

The fire god

The last child birthed by Izanami was Hi-no-Kagutsuchi, the god of fire. However, as she delivered him, the fire god burned Izanami's genitals, causing her to dispel bodily fluids, which turned into more islands and deities. Tragically, Izanami died from her injuries. Enraged by her death, her husband Izanagi

IZANAGI'S LEGACY

The wooden gate at the entrance to Izanagi Shrine on the island of Awaji.

Izanagi has been called a 'transitional' figure as the last generation of the creation gods as well as the father of the earthly world. He is often portrayed as a fierce, bearded, middle-aged man with a spear.

Some of the shrines that worship him as their chief deity include Izanagi Shrine in Awaji City, Hyōgo Prefecture, the supposed location of the god's palace after his retirement and subsequently his tomb. Both Izanagi and Izanami are enshrined here. Awaji Island is said to be the first island created by the primal pair, then referred to as Onogoro. Taga Grand Shrine in Shiga Prefecture and Eda Shrine in Miyazaki Prefecture are also dedicated to the couple.

LEFT: **The sacred Meoto Iwa, or Married Couple Rocks, at Futami Okitama Shrine off the coast of Ise, Mie Prefecture, represent the union of Izanagi and Izanami.**

took his anger out on the fire child, slicing him with his sword and killing him; the blood and entrails that spilled from the child and coated Izanagi's mighty blade became more spirits, those of volcanoes and storms.

Journey to the underworld

After his wife's death, Izanagi sought to rejoin her, and so he followed her to Yomi, the underworld and land of the dead. There, he met with Izanami in a great hall and entreated her to return with him. She agreed, provided that the spirits of the underworld gave their permission, and so she went to speak with them. She asked only that Izanagi not look upon her as she did so. Izanagi, however, soon grew impatient waiting, and peeked inside the hall; there, he saw his beautiful wife turned to a rotten, maggot-infested corpse. Horrified, he fled from this awful sight.

The maggots slithering through Izanami's body turned into thunder spirits that she sent in pursuit of her husband, along with other hideous creatures from the underworld. As they chased him, Izanagi threw down the combs from his hair as distractions until only Izanami remained chasing him. When he reached the entrance to the underworld, he rolled a huge boulder to block her

IZANAMI'S LEGACY

Although Izanami became a resident of the underworld in the narrative told in the *Kojiki*, she is usually depicted and worshipped as a goddess of life, marriage and motherhood. After all, she is a creator god first and foremost.

Hananoiwaya Shrine in Kumamo City, Mie Prefecture, is located at a cave called the Flower Cavern that is said to be Izanami's grave and the entrance to the underworld land of Yomi. It is one of the oldest shrines in Japan, and although it is a Shinto shrine, it is also part of Buddhist history. Although its exact founding date is unknown, mention of it is made in the *Nihon Shoki*.

The object of worship on the site is a 45-m (148-ft) high boulder said to be the rock that Izanagi used to block the entrance to Yomi. Attached to the boulder is a sacred *shimenawa* rope that extends for 170m (550ft). Twice a year, locals gather for a rope-changing ceremony during which they pull on the rope: if the rope breaks, it is replaced; if it stays strong, a new one is placed next to it. The presence of two ropes is considered a sign of good luck.

Shrine-goers performing the ritual to change the sacred straw rope at Hananoiwaya Shrine in Kumano, Mie Prefecture.

way. The couple talked through the barrier of the boulder, and decided that they were now separated, signifying what could be the world's first divorce. Izanami vowed that she would kill 1000 mortals each day; in retaliation, Izanagi proclaimed that he would ensure that 1500 new births occurred daily.

Gods of the natural world

Upon emerging from the underworld, Izanagi felt the need to cleanse its foul remnants from his body. As he discarded each item of dress, they turned into deities. The same happened as he washed each part of his body. Some of these *kami* were pure and some were polluted by the dregs of the underworld. Izanagi was especially pleased with the last three child gods who came from him, and to these he assigned dominions to rule over. They were Amaterasu, to whom he assigned the rule of Heaven and the sun, Tsukiyomi, to whom he assigned the rule of night and the moon, and Susano-wo, to whom he assigned the rule of the sea.

BELOW: **Amaterasu the sun goddess emerges from the cave in this woodblock print by Kunisada (1786–1865).**

An alternative narrative

The story above is that of Japan's creation as told in the *Kojiki*. However, the *Nihon Shoki* portrays a much happier version of events: Izanami does not die, and instead births the three celestial gods herself before retiring together with her husband. Regardless of the story's version, the main point of the creator gods handing rule of their creation over to their three children remains the same.

The Celestial Gods

Once the islands of Japan had been created and the celestial gods established in their respective domains, it was time for the next generation to take up the mantle.

Amaterasu

The sun goddess Amaterasu is perhaps the most important figure in all Japanese mythology. Her name translates as 'Heaven Shining', and after being born from the primal couple, she ruled over the High Plain of Heaven. She sits at

the head of all the eight million Shinto *kami* and is the direct ancestor of the imperial house, making every Japanese person her indirect descendant.

Using the *honji-suijaku* theory, some Buddhist sects have claimed her as an avatar of the sun bodhisattva, Dainichi Nyorai, whereas in the 16th century she became associated with the Buddhist goddess, Kannon.

The main shrine dedicated to Amaterasu is Ise Shrine in Mie Prefecture, one of the most important shrines in Japan. The main shrine buildings are torn down and rebuilt every 20 years from plain cypress wood. It is a cyclical process, with almost a decade dedicated to planning, followed by another 10 years of construction. The inner sanctum supposedly holds the Sacred Mirror of the Imperial Regalia, although it is strictly hidden from public access.

Tsukuyomi

As the *Nihon Shoki* tells it, in the beginning, Amaterasu and Tsukuyomi worked together in the sky. One day, Tsukuyomi visited the lands below. He encountered Ukemochi, the goddess of food, who produced sustenance from her bodily

Cosmological geography

Takamagahara
Translated as 'The High Plain of Heaven', this is the heavenly realm where the *amatsukami* reside.

Ashihara-no-Nakatsukuni
This is the Central Land of the Reed Plains – the earthly realm where the *kunitsukami* dwell.

The Floating Bridge of Heaven
This bridge where Izanagi and Izanami stood to stir the gelatinous land with the heavenly spear. It connects the domains of Heaven and Earth.

Yomi
The underworld.

orifices. Thinking that she was disrespecting him by giving him fouled food produced from an impure part of herself, Tsukuyomi killed her. For this, Amaterasu banished him from her domain, forever condemning the sun and the moon to wander the skies separately, the moon at night and the sun in the day. Rice, wheat and more were found in the body of the slain goddess, and Amaterasu declared that these would be used to sustain humanity. This story is, however, absent from the *Kojiki*: there, it is Susano-wo who is the villain and who kills a similar food goddess.

Overall, Tsukuyomi is the neglected sibling of the celestial trio, who rarely appears in later myths, stories or art, and is usually only worshipped at smaller shrines that are part of larger complexes honoring Amaterasu. One of these is the Tsukuyomi Shrine in Mie Prefecture, an outer shrine of Ise Shrine, the grand shrine that enshrines his sister Amaterasu.

ABOVE: **The god Susano-wo by printmaker Yoshitoshi Tsukioka (1839–1892).**

Susano-wo

Originally assigned rule of the sea, Susano-wo is a complex and contradictory figure, famous both as a villain and a hero. He is a wild, uncontrollable force, as we will see in the story of his rampage and subsequent banishment, yet in his encounter with the eight-forked serpent and other legends, he proves his mettle as a hero and slayer of monsters. After his banishment, he becomes the ruler of the underworld of Yomi.

ABOVE: **Vibrant floats parade the streets during the Gion Matsuri in Kyoto.**

There is also a surprisingly sensitive side to him, as he is credited with composing the world's first poem:

Many clouds arise,
On all sides a manifold fence,
To receive within it the spouses,
They form a manifold fence:
Ah! That manifold fence!
– translation by W. G. Aston

Connected with the sea, tempests and pestilence, Susano-wo is invoked to protect against calamity and disease, and there are many shrines dedicated to him as a patron of various things. In Izumo there are Susa Shrine and Yaegaki Shrine, as well as Suga Shrine, which is said to stand on the site where Susano-wo was inspired to recite the above poem and subsequently built his palace and lived with his new wife after defeating the serpent.

Susano-wo is associated with the syncretic deity Gozu Tennō, a deity of disease and healing. Yasaka Shrine in Kyoto's Gion district is dedicated to appeasing the god of pestilence, which for a long time meant both Susano-wo and Gozu Tennō as Shinto and Buddhist aspects of the same deity, before becoming dedicated solely to Susano-wo with the state separation of Buddhism and Shinto during the Meiji era (1868–1912). Built in the 7th century, Yasaka enjoyed imperial patronage in the Heian period (794–1192) and was a first rank, government-supported shrine (*kanpei-taisha*) during the Meiji period. The Gion Festival, held in July, is one of Japan's biggest and most famous. It is a riot of music, colour and food, with the huge *yamaboko* floats being the main draw.

Susano-wo's rampage

The role of villain in this myth falls to Susano-wo. While his brother and sister happily assumed rule of their respective domains, Susano-wo immediately abandoned his duties and instead spent his time wandering around wailing and crying. When his father took him to task, Susano-wo complained that he missed his mother. Furious, Izanagi banished him from the seas. Some accounts say that he was sent to the underworld of Yomi, whereas others tell that he fled to the High Plain of Heaven to seek out his sister Amaterasu.

When she learned of her brother's approach, Amaterasu was suspicious of his intentions. She armed and armored herself and tied her hair up in a masculine fashion. When Susano-wo arrived, she performed a war dance to show that she was not to be trifled with. She did not trust her brother, but he persuaded her to put him to the test by making children with him.

So, the two made oaths to one another, then Amaterasu took her brother's sword, broke it into three pieces, rinsed the pieces, then chewed them and spat them out. Three deities sprang forth from the spray as she spat. Then Susano-wo took the pendants from each side of her hair and around her arms. These he rinsed and chewed and spat, and his spray brought forth five deities. The accounts now differ as to whether Amaterasu conceded defeat because the male deities came from her brother's possessions, or

CONNECTED WITH THE SEA, TEMPESTS AND PESTILENCE, SUSANO-WO IS INVOKED TO PROTECT AGAINST CALAMITY AND DISEASE, AND THERE ARE MANY SHRINES DEDICATED TO HIM.

whether Susano-wo won fair and square, proving his innocent intent because the first children were male. Either way, Susano-wo was victorious and allowed into his sister's domain. However, he immediately betrayed Amaterasu's hospitality by going on a rampage, destroying the rice paddies and defecating in her hall. The good-natured Amaterasu excused his behaviour but soon came to regret it as his disrespect only grew more flagrant. One day, Susano-wo skinned a pony backwards and threw it through the roof of the weaving hall, where the shock caused a weaver deity to hit herself in the genitals with her shuttle and die. This was the last straw for Amaterasu – disgusted and fearful, she withdrew to a cave where she shut herself away from the world.

Amaterasu and the cave

After the sun goddess sequestered herself in the cave, the world was thrown into chaos: eternal night covered the land and the heavens, and many calamities arose. The eight million *kami*

BELOW: **The gods watch Uzume no Mikoto as she dances to lure the sun goddess Amaterasu out of her cave. Unknown artist, circa 1880.**

THE IMPERIAL REGALIA

Kusanagi-no-Tsurugi
The sacred sword that represents valour.

Yata-no-Kagami
The mirror that represents wisdom and in which Amaterasu glimpsed her reflection.

Yasakani-no-Magatama
The jewel that represents benevolence, which was used to lure Amaterasu from the cave.

A staff member carries a cloth-wrapped box containing one of the imperial regalia at Emperor Akihito's abdication ceremony on April 30, 2019.

Although these three objects supposedly exist in reality, they are never shown to the public. They make their appearance only in closed boxes during the ascension of a new emperor to the throne. This last happened in 2019 when Emperor Akihito abdicated and his son, Naruhito, took the throne, marking the end of the Heisei era (1989–2019) and the start of Reiwa.

gathered together to discuss how to remedy the situation. Taking the special materials needed, they had some *kami* fashion a metal mirror and long strings of beads. Then they uprooted a sacred tree and replanted it in front of the cavern, where they hung it with the mirror, jewels and offerings. Appropriate rituals were performed and prayers intoned.

Then, the deity Ama-no-uzume kicked over a bucket and clambered atop it, tying up her hair and sleeves. She began a bawdy dance, exposing her breasts and genitals. The gathered *kami* laughed and guffawed.

Within the cave, Amaterasu heard the laughter and grew curious as to why the *kami* were laughing when all the Heavens

ABOVE: **Susano-wo slays the eight-headed serpent Yamata no Orochi. Woodblock print by Yoshitoshi Tsukioka (1839–1892), now housed in the Philadelphia Museum of Art.**

were covered in darkness without her light? She pushed the boulder to reveal a crack, peered out and demanded to know what all the noise was about.

'We laugh because we have here a *kami* even more magnificent than you!' they cried.

With her attention caught, two deities took the mirror and showed it to Amaterasu so that she could see her own reflection. Even more intrigued, the sun goddess began to slowly creep out of the cave, at which point a strong and mighty deity who had been lying in wait grabbed her hand and pulled her fully out of the cave mouth. Behind her, a ritual expert closed up the cave and bound it with a sacred rope, declaring that never again could she enter the cave. Thus, the sun goddess' radiance brought light back to the lands.

As punishment, Susano-wo had his beard shaved and nails plucked and was exiled. He was sent down to Earth where he arrived in the land of Izumo.

Susano-wo and the serpent

As the exiled god wandered the land of Izumo, he came across a *kami* couple who had borne eight daughters. Tragically, seven of them had been eaten, one per year, by the eight-tailed serpent Yamata-no-Orochi, and it was almost time for it to come and take the eighth. Susano-wo magnanimously offered to help them by slaying the dragon – if, however, he could have the eighth daughter's hand in marriage in return.

Before this happened, Susano-wo changed his potential future bride, whose name was Kushinada-hime, into a comb that he then stuck into his hair for safekeeping. Next, he asked the old couple to brew gallons of sake and instructed them to construct a large fence with eight gates, and behind each gate a platform. Atop these platforms were set vats filled with the sake.

When the great serpent with its eight heads and eight tails, as long as eight hills and eight valleys, came slithering slowly to collect the eighth daughter, it was distracted by the sake. Each head drank deeply of the vats until the snake fell into a drunken sleep, at which point Susano-wo leaped out and chopped it to pieces.

As he sliced through one of the tails, his sword struck something. Digging into the tail, he found a great sword that later became known as Kusanagi-no-Tsurugi. This sword he presented to Amaterasu by way of an apology for his previous behaviour.

BELOW: **Izumo Grand Shrine in Shimane is one of the oldest and most important Shinto shrines in Japan.**

ONE OF SUSANO-
WO'S MANY
DESCENDENTES,
EITHER DIRECT
OR DISTANT
DEPENDING ON
THE VERSION, WAS
ŌKINONUSHI, THE
ORIGINAL 'MASTER
OF THE LAND'.

With the creature slain, Susano-wo turned Kushinada-hime back into human form, married her and built a palace for her at Suga, although he would also have many more wives.

Ōkuninushi

One of Susano-wo's many descendants, either direct or distant depending on the version, was Ōkuninushi, the original ruler of the Earth, whose name translates to 'master of the land'. After surviving various assassination attempts by his brothers and overcoming Susano-wo's trials in order to marry the god's daughter Suseribime, Ōkuninushi became ruler of the land and head of the earthly gods, or *kunitsukami*. He continued with the process of creating the land that Izanami and Izanagi had started, and as such he is seen as calming the forces of nature. His syncretic Buddhist deity is Daikokuten, one of the seven lucky gods.

The Izumo Grand Shrine was supposedly presented to Ōkuninushi by Amaterasu after he passed on the land to Ninigi, and Ōkuninushi is worshipped there as an ancestral guardian *kami* and deity of the connections between people. The Kamiari Festival is held annually on the tenth month of the lunar calendar and welcomes the gods for their yearly convention. Around Izumo, October is referred to as *kamiarizuki*, or the 'month with the gods', whereas in the rest of Japan it is *kannazuki*, 'the month without gods'.

The white hare of Inaba

Ōkuninushi had 80 brothers who all wished to marry the beautiful Princess Yagami of Inaba. They set out on a journey to woo her, taking their youngest brother Ōkuninushi along to carry the baggage.

On the way, they came across a skinned hare sprawled on the ground. The brothers thought it would be a hilarious jape to tell the hare to bathe in the sea then lie exposed to the winds on a high peak. The hare did this, and its skin blistered and cracked, and it cried in pain.

When Ōkuninushi, who had been taking up the rear, came to the hare, he asked it why it was crying. The hare told him how it had wanted to cross over to the mainland from an island. Having no way to do so on its own, it tricked a sea beast into helping.

'I told the beast that we should have a contest to see whose clan is larger; the hares or the sea beasts. I said that I would count its kin if they would all gather and form a line from the island to the cape. This they did, and I ran across the bridge they formed, counting as I went; but when I was almost at the land, I cried out in glee that I had tricked them. The last beast in the line snapped at me and tore my fur coat from my body.'

The hare recounted how Ōkuninushi's 80 brothers had told it what to do, which resulted in its current sorry state. Ōkuninushi told the hare to wash in fresh water then roll in the pollen of a particular plant. The hare did as instructed, and its body was healed.

BELOW: **Statues of Okuninushi and the Hare of Inaba at Jishujinja Shrine in Kyoto.**

'For this, you will be the one to marry Princess Yagami, not any of your 80 brothers, the hare told Ōkuninushi.

And when they arrived, this proved true, for Princess Yagami had eyes only for Ōkuninushi, and the two were quickly married. Naturally, Ōkuninushi had several other wives as well as many dalliances, and Princess Yagami would later be replaced as chief wife by another, as we shall find out later.

Assassination attempts

After being rejected by Princess Yagami, Ōkuninushi's brothers were enraged and sought revenge. Together, they conspired to kill their brother. First, they invited Ōkuninushi to come hunting with them at Mount Tema. They had him wait at the foot of the mountain, towards which they would drive the red boar they pursued. This, however, was a lie – instead of a boar, they sent a huge boulder heated to lethal temperatures rolling down the slope. When he grabbed the rock, Ōkuninushi was burned to

BELOW: **A priest strikes a large drum during worship at Izumo Grand Shrine.**

death. Distraught, his mother ascended to Heaven to petition Kamimusibu to restore her son to life. He granted her request and sent two goddesses to not only revive him, but to bring him back as a handsome young man.

The brothers seethed with anger that their plan had been foiled but vowed to try again. For their next attempt, they split open a tree, tricked Ōkuninushi to walk between the two sides, then removed the wedges that had been keeping it open, squashing their poor brother between them. Once again, his mother revived him but this time told him to flee. Ōkuninushi's brothers pursued him, but he managed to dodge them and slip away, after which he set out to seek counsel with his ancestor Susano-wo.

Trials and tribulations

Ōkuninushi went to Susano-wo where he was staying in the Land of Roots. There he met Susano-wo's daughter, Suseribime. Being a passionate man, Ōkuninushi quickly fell for her, but Susano-wo was not going to hand his daughter over to just anyone; he arranged for four trials to test the young god.

For the first trial, Ōkuninushi was made to sleep in a room full of snakes. Suseribime gave her lover a special scarf that repelled the snakes, and he survived the night.

For the second trial, Susano-wo made Ōkuninushi sleep in a room of centipedes and bees. Again, Suseribime gave him a scarf that protected him from the insects.

For the third trial, Susano-wo shot an arrow and sent Ōkuninushi to retrieve it. As Ōkuninushi searched the field, Susano-wo set fire to the grass. Fortunately for Ōkuninushi, a helpful mouse led him to a hole where he hid until the fire burned out. The mouse even brought the arrow to him.

Lastly, Susano-wo invited the still-living Ōkuninushi to pick lice from his head, which would have been an intimate gesture. However, Ōkuninushi found the deity's head to be crawling with poisonous centipedes. Still, he managed to trick the elder god into thinking he was chewing up and spitting out the deadly creatures, and thus demonstrated his strength.

Eventually, Susano-wo fell asleep, and Ōkuninushi took this opportunity to tie the deity's hair to the rafters and block the door to his chamber with a large rock. Then he took Susano-wo's sword, bow and arrows, and *koto* stringed instrument, along with his daughter Suseribime, and fled. The sound of them leaving woke Susano-wo, who leaped up only to pull the entire building down upon himself, preventing him from giving chase.

Now deeming Ōkuninushi worthy of his daughter's hand in marriage, Susano-wo gave his blessing and bade Ōkuninushi to use the stolen weapons to subdue his brothers and to build a great palace. Ōkuninushi promptly did so, then set about the task of finishing creating the land. During this, he had many more passionate affairs that resulted in many offspring.

Pacifying the land

Eventually, Ōkuninushi finished creating the land and fixed it so that it could support crops. However, all was still not well.

The *amatsukami* up in Heaven saw that the land below was chaotic and rife with disturbances, and they gathered to discuss what to do about the situation. The decision they came to was that the land below must be pacified and united with Heaven under the rule of the heavenly gods instead of the earthly.

Now began the process of putting this plan into action. Three gods were sent down to Earth in succession, but one by one, each became distracted and failed to do as they had been instructed.

Eventually, Takemikazuchi, one of the gods birthed when Izanagi slayed the fire god, was sent and success was achieved via negotiations with Ōkuninushi and his council. In the end, Ōkuninushi agreed to hand over rule of the Earth in return for a great palace in Izumo, special food, and direct access to Heaven.

At long last, the *amatsukami* had dominion over creation and all was ready for the August Grandchild to descend.

Ninigi

Known by many names, Ninigi is Amaterasu's direct descendant who was sent to the earthly realm to rule on behalf of the *amatsukami* in Heaven. Although there are few shrines dedicated to him, he is an important deity as ancestor of the imperial clan that would go on to rule Japan. The escort of other deities who descended to Earth with Ninigi would also go on to become

OPPOSITE: **Takemikazuchi holds down a catfish in this woodblock print featuring an earthquake-warding song. Catfish, or** *namazu,* **were believed to either cause or predict earthquakes.**

the ancestors of other prominent clans. Kirishima Shrine in Kagoshima Prefecture is located at the foot of Mount Takachiho, the peak in the Kirishima mountain range where the heavenly cohort are said to have landed.

Before Ninigi descended, Amaterasu gave him the three Imperial Regalia: the sword, the mirror and the jewel, which have supposedly been passed down through the imperial line until the present day.

From gods to emperors

On Earth, Ninigi met the beautiful Princess Konohanasakuya, whose name means 'flower blossom'. Her father was Oyamatsumi, a god of the mountains, and Ninigi soon sought his blessing to marry the princess. Oyamatsumi was delighted by the proposal and also sent his other daughter Princess Iwanaga, whose name means 'long-rock', to Ninigi. However, Ninigi was disgusted by the elder sister's ugliness and sent her back.

BELOW: **Kirishima Shrine in Kagoshima Prefecture stands on the site where Ninigi is said to have descended to earth.**

The mountain god was angered and humiliated by this rejection. He revealed to Ninigi that he had sent Iwanaga so that Ninigi and his descendants' lives would be as long as the rocks, and that his other daughter would ensure their lives flourish as the tree blossoms.

'But since you have rejected Iwanaga, your life shall be as fleeting as the blossoms.'

From that day, the emperors of Japan were doomed to live short lives, at least in comparison to the lifespans of the gods.

After just one night together as newlyweds, Konohanasakuya became pregnant. Finding this highly suspicious, Ninigi accused her of infidelity, but she proved her innocence by setting her birthing hut on fire – or Ninigi set it aflame, depending on the myth version. When she and the baby came through the flames unharmed, Ninigi was placated. The couple's most well-known children are Hoderi and Hoori, their names meaning 'bright flame' and 'flickering flame' respectively.

Hoderi and Hoori

The story of the brothers Hoderi and Hoori is a familiar one of sibling rivalry. Hoderi was a deity of the sea and so could catch any fish; Hoori was a deity of the mountains, and as such could catch any game. Hoori kept pestering his brother to exchange fortunes, until his elder brother finally relented. Yet even with his brother's fortune, Hoori could not catch a single fish. He also lost the special fish hook that Hoderi had lent him in the sea.

When Hoderi said they should switch their fortunes back and asked for his fish hook, Hoori admitted that he had lost it. He tried to make up for it by breaking up his mighty sword and fashioning it into 500 new fishhooks, but his elder brother insisted on having his original hook back.

As Hoderi sulked on the seashore, he received advice from a passing deity, which he followed. He took a coracle and went out to sea until he reached the scaled palace of the *kami* of the sea, where he then climbed a sacred laurel tree by the gate. When the princess' serving girl came out to draw water from the well, she saw Hoderi reflected in her pitcher. He asked for a drink, then took a jewel from around his neck, coated it with his saliva and

BEFORE NINIGI DESCENDED, AMATERASU GAVE HIM THE THREE IMPERIAL REGALIA: THE SWORD, THE MIRROR AND THE JEWEL, WHICH HAVE SUPPOSEDLY BEEN PASSED DOWN THROUGH THE IMPERIAL LINE UNTIL THE PRESENT DAY.

dropped it into the pitcher where it became lodged. She brought this back to the princess Toyotama who, intrigued, went out to look up into the tree for herself, whereupon she fell in love with the handsome Hoderi at first sight. The two were soon married.

After three years of wedded bliss, Hoderi began to feel homesick and told his father-in-law the story of how he had ended up there. At once, Owatatsumi called for all the fish in the sea to see if any of them had found the lost fish hook, and it was discovered lodged in the throat of a sea bream. Owatatsumi instructed Hoderi in a curse to bring bad luck to whoever bore the hook, telling him, 'If your brother builds his rice paddies high, then build yours low. As lord of the water, I can deprive his high fields or flood his low ones, and he will soon become a poor man.'

He also gave Hoderi two jewels, saying, 'If he attacks you, use the tide-raising jewel to drown him; if he is penitent and begs for forgiveness, use the tide-ebbing jewel to revive him.' Then he sent Hoderi home on a sea beast.

Following this advice, Hoderi wore his brother down until Hoori attacked him, at which point he used the tide-raising jewel to drown him. On the verge of drowning, Hoori begged for his life and Hoderi obliged, this time using the tide-ebbing jewel. Defeated, Hoori pledged that he and his descendants would forever serve his brother Hoderi.

The first emperor

Ninigi's earthly lineage leads directly to the first emperor of Japan – the Hoori mentioned above is his grandfather. The first emperor's name is Jimmu, meaning 'the weapon of the gods'. In his blood runs the divine right to rule over all creation; he represents the unity of ruling forces with divine authority from Amaterasu, as well as claims over the land and the *kunitsukami*, and over the sea.

This represents a clear shift from heavenly concerns to earthly, with the chronicles now focusing on human emperors who spend their time ruling over mortal matters on the firmament. Nonetheless, the first 15 or so emperors are considered legendary, with no historical evidence to back up their existence, and their

NINIGI'S EARTHLY LINEAGE LEADS DIRECTLY TO THE FIRST EMPEROR OF JAPAN... THE FIRST EMPEROR'S NAME IS JIMMU, MEANING 'THE WEAPON OF THE GODS'.

stories are just as fantastical as those of the preceding deities.

The young prince grew up with his three brothers in Himuka, located in the southernmost island now known as Kyushu. One day, Jimmu encountered a local *kunitsukami* named Shiotsuchi who told him of a vision he had in which Amaterasu instructed him that the princes should travel north to find Yamato, a fertile area of mountain-ringed land that would become the centre of the realm once the unruly *kunitsukami* there were quelled.

Jimmu and his brother Itsuse took this to heart and set out together on a journey to find Yamato with various other deities in tow, depending on the version. Amaterasu also sent down a giant crow to guide them. On the way, the group made numerous stops where they were opposed by *tsuchigumo*, a spider-like monster. They either won the *tsuchigumo* over to their side or fought them to emerge victorious.

When the group reached Naniwa, present-day Osaka, they took a boat, but were quickly set upon by Nagasunebiko, the lord of Yamato. During the battle, Itsuse was struck by an arrow and died soon after. Jimmu then set sail south to Kumano, present-day Shingu in Wakayama. Back on land, he received a favorable omen and he and his army moved on, journeying through the mountains of the Kii Peninsula along an ancient pilgrimage route called the Kumano Kodō.

ABOVE: **Yoshitoshi Tsukioka's print shows Emperor Jimmu with his simple bow, atop which a golden kite landed after one of his military victories.**

When they came face to face with Nagasunebiko's forces on the gentle slopes of Mount Kaguyama, Jimmu and his army easily defeated them. This battle is barely a brief note in the *Kojiki*, whereas the *Nihon Shoki* provides additional stories of subterfuge.

Following his pacification of Yamato, Emperor Jimmu, first emperor of Japan, was enthroned on 11 February 660BCE. The Meiji government designated 11 February as National Foundation Day. It was removed as a national holiday following World War II, then reinstated in 1966. Today, Kashihara Shrine in Nara Prefecture purports to sit atop the site of where Emperor Jimmu's palace was built.

The divine right to rule

The mythology of the Japanese imperial line has been an important tool for Japan's rulers since the Yamato clan first sought to exert its dominance. As mentioned at the beginning of this chapter, the 'official histories' recorded in the *Kojiki* and *Nihon Shoki* are understood to have been the ancient court's way of legitimizing their authority through cementing their divine lineage.

BELOW: **The great wooden *torii* gate at Kashihara Shrine in Nara Prefecture. It is left unpainted because the shrine is dedicated to a member of the imperial household, Emperor Jimmu. The previous gate stood for 80 years before being renovated in 2020.**

Although the emperor is the metaphysical centre of the realm, the actual influence of the emperor has waxed and waned over time. With the emperor's position as the earthly connection to the heavenly *kami*, much of their duty was, and still remains, ceremonial and ritual-based. While some took decisive action, just as many were sequestered away while actual rule was undertaken by others, such as the shogunate during the Edo period (1603–1868).

The most recent resurgence of imperial myth being used for political purpose was during the lead up to World War II. Following the Meiji Restoration of 1868, a system now referred to as State Shinto was implemented under the new government, by which Shinto beliefs and practices were incorporated into a patriotic national ideology, called *kokutai*. To encourage unity and dedication to the imperial state among the people, the emperor's divine origin was taught in schools as historical fact rather than myth, and the emperor himself was to be worshipped as a god. This lasted until Japan's defeat in 1945 and the implementation of the post-war constitution.

On 1 January 1946, Emperor Hirohito issued an imperial rescript renouncing the 'conception that the Emperor is divine' and stating that the nation was not built upon myths. Article 1 of the Constitution of Japan, introduced in 1947, states that 'The Emperor shall be the symbol of the State and of the unity of the People, deriving his position from the will of the people with whom resides sovereign power.'

Japanese eras are still named for the emperor, with a new era ending when an emperor dies or is removed from the throne and beginning when a new one ascends. The current era, which began in 2019 with the ascension of Emperor Naruhito, is named the Reiwa, which roughly translates to 'beautiful harmony'.

Imperial legacy

Emperor Jimmu apparently ruled for 76 years, until he was around 160 or 170 years old. Upon his death, he was entombed in the first Imperial Mausoleum, although no burial mound has been found in the region where this is supposed to be. This has led to much debate among scholars as to whether Jimmu was a real person

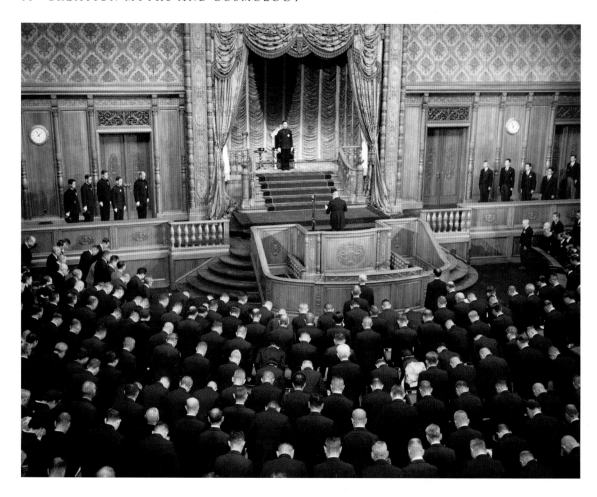

ABOVE: **The Constitution of Japan is signed on November 3rd, 1946. The new constitution renounced the myth of the emperor's divinity and placed sovereignty with the people.**

or entirely fictional. Indeed, the historical existence of many of the first emperors recorded in the chronicles is up for debate, with only the later figures after the first 15 being proven through extant contemporary historical documents and finds to be based on real people. Modern scholars refer to the earlier group as the 'legendary' emperors, but that is not to say that they have always been regarded as such.

Despite this, in mythological terms, with the first emperor the transition from the age of the heavenly gods to that of mortals and the earthly realm is complete. Rather than heavenly affairs, the 'ancient matters' recorded in the chronicles now shift to records of each emperor's rule.

Nonetheless, even in subsequent times there is no shortage of *kami*, spirits, heroes and mythological beings populating the islands of Japan, as the following chapters will show.

RYUKYUAN CREATION MYTHS

The *Chūzan Seikan* was compiled by Shō Shōken in 1650 and is the first official history of the Ryukyu Kingdom. Similar to the *Kojiki* and *Nihon Shoki*, it details the land's creation myths, which have many similarities with those of Japan, and provides an official court mythology that may deviate heavily from the folk beliefs of the general populace at the time.

The Heavenly Emperor lived in the Heavenly Gusuku, a gusuku being a type of stone-walled castle specific to the Ryukyu Islands. One day he sent down a brother and sister pair of kang, Shinerikyu and Amamikyu, to create the land and the people who would live upon it. They descended from heaven and set about creating Kudaka Island, a paradise rich in earth, trees and flowers. Amamikyu also built Tamagusuku Castle, the oldest castle on Okinawa, and Chinen Castle, the second oldest. There are differing accounts of how many children they had, but it is generally understood that these offspring represented the different classes of Ryukyuan society: rulers, priestesses and farmers. The sacred area of Sefa-utaki is said to be where Amamikyu first descended from Heaven; it rose to spiritual prominence in the early 16th century when the indigenous religion was centralized and restructured under the royal government.

The Tamagusuku castle ruins in Okinawa are the oldest on the island. The castle was said to have been built by the creation goddesss Amamikyu.

2

KAMI – OTHER SPIRITS AND DEITIES

The Japanese term *kami* is somewhat difficult to translate into English – the closest equivalent would probably be 'deity'. Generally speaking, a *kami* is a powerful spiritual being that can intervene in human affairs. They run the gamut from vague, unspecified and non-personalized concentrations of power to personalized deities with names, personalities and distinct attributes.

This vast array of *kami* is sometimes referred to in the Shinto tradition as *yaoyorozu-no-kamigami*, or the eight million deities. *Kami* are often associated with natural phenomena or embodied within them, for example, within an inspiring-looking rock or natural water feature. Real historical figures can also be deified as *kami* – an equivalent could be drawn to people receiving sainthood in Christian traditions – and the gods of other religions, such as the Christian God, would also be referred to with the term *kami*. For this reason, the terms 'god', 'deity' and '*kami*' will be used interchangeably throughout this chapter.

OPPOSITE: A celebratory dance to Jurojin, one of the Taoist gods of fortune, at Mount Kaimon in Satsuma Province (from a woodcut by Utagawa Hiroshige II, 1859).

ABOVE: **Motoori Norinaga (1730–1801) was one of the leading scholars of the Edo period. He is known as one of the Four Great Men of *Kokugaku*, or nativist studies.**

Motoori Norinaga, a scholar of the Edo period (1603–1868), summed his thoughts on *kami* up as follows: 'I do not yet understand the meaning of the word "*kami*". In the most general sense, it refers to all divine beings of heaven and earth that appear in the classics. More particularly, the *kami* are the spirits that abide in and are worshipped at the shrines.'

The worship of *kami* is fluid and non-restrictive, with some deities enshrined in sprawling shrine complexes, while others are known only to small local communities or even individual households. If a *kami* is sufficiently honoured and the correct rituals performed, they can help and protect those who call upon them. Purity attracts *kami* whereas pollution repels them, and many Shinto rituals are rituals of purification. Some *kami* are worshipped within both Shinto and Buddhism, and some only by specific faiths or sects; many are important not only to religious believers but to ostensibly secular people also, as an ingrained part of Japanese culture.

There is an incredibly diverse range of *kami*, from native Shinto deities to imports from China and India, from gods with completely mystical origins to those with a basis in real historical figures who were later deified. Below we will take a look at a few of the major *kami* from the expansive Japanese pantheon.

FESTIVALS

One of the ways that mythology is kept alive for modern Japanese people is through festivals, called *matsuri* in Japanese. These traditional events are a mainstay of national and local calendars. Many festivals are clustered around the traditional holidays of Setsubun at the end of winter and Obon in midsummer, or in the autumn celebration of the rice harvest. The traditions observed depend on the type of festival and the area where it is held, but they are usually fun and sociable affairs with stalls selling street food and offering carnival games for children, and people performing traditional dance and music. Often, a local *kami* will be enshrined within a *mikoshi*, or portable shrine, and carried through the streets in a procession. With many festivals, the participants' degree of religiosity varies greatly, similar to how Christmas is now celebrated both religiously and secularly in Western countries.

Held in July during the oppressive summer heat, the Gion Festival fills the streets of central Kyoto with vibrant floats, traditional music and dance, and delicious street food.

Kannon

Kannon, or Kanzeon Bosatsu, is one of the most popular goddesses worshipped in Japan and is a perfect example of the dizzying blend of influences and belief systems within Japanese mythology. In simple terms, Kannon is the Japanese incarnation of a bodhisattva called Avalokiteshvara in Sanskrit. After being imported from India to China (and changing gender along the way) she was reinterpreted as Guanyin before making her way to Japan with the introduction of Buddhism. She is paired with Amaterasu as her Shinto counterpart and is also associated with the Virgin Mary; when Christianity was outlawed in Japan during the Edo period, statues of Mary were substituted by those of Kannon holding a child in order to evade the ban. In this form, she is referred to as Maria Kannon. After much transformation following her introduction as a bodhisattva, Kannon is now firmly entrenched within the diverse Japanese pantheon and can sometimes be spotted in surprising places; for example, the name of Canon, Inc., the multinational camera company, originated from the name of the goddess.

Often portrayed as a slim female figure, Kannon is a goddess of compassion and mercy. In recent times, as Japan grapples with the realities of an ageing population, she has taken on an association with senility, and people pray to her to ward off dementia.

There are both Buddhist temples and Shinto shrines dedicated to Kannon in her various forms. Nowhere is this symbiosis more obvious than in Asakusa, Tokyo. There you can find Sensō-ji, a Buddhist temple dedicated to Kannon and one of Japan's most famous tourist spots, while right next to it is the Asakusa Shrine, a Shinto shrine that honors the three founders of Sensō-ji as *kami*.

The story goes that in 628, two fishermen found a statuette of Kannon in the Sumida River. When a local wealthy man heard this, he went to the two men and spoke passionately of the Buddha, after which they promptly converted to Buddhism. The men enshrined the statue in a small temple, which would go on to become Sensō-ji, the oldest temple in Tokyo. The shrine was commissioned in 1694 by Tokugawa Iemitsu.

At 100m (328ft) tall, Sendai Daikannon is the fifth-tallest statue in the world and depicts the goddess as a white-robed

OPPOSITE: **The bodhisattva Kannon is shown in a white robe, painted by Sakai Hōitsu (1761–1828), an artist and Buddhist monk.**

BELOW: **Sensō-ji is the oldest Buddhist temple in Tokyo and is dedicated to the bodhisattva Kannon.**

Kannon holding a cintamani wish-fulfilling gem. Meanwhile in Kyoto, the Sanjūsangen-dō Temple ('Temple of 33 Bays') houses 1001 statues of the Thousand-Armed Kannon; 1000 of these are life-sized statues that stand guard around the main deity, which was sculpted in the Kamakura period (1192–1333). The number 33 is considered sacred to Kannon, and she is believed to have 33 forms. The Saigoku Kannon Pilgrimage takes place through the Kansai area and stops at 33 Buddhist temples dedicated to the different versions of Kannon.

Origins of the Saigoku Pilgrimage

In 718 Tokudo Shonin, the Buddhist priest who founded Hasedera Temple, lay dying from illness. As he slipped from this world, he found himself in the palace of King Enma, Lord of the Dead. Tokudo saw that the room sparkled with gold and jewels, and the king himself appeared to be glowing with a brilliant light. The dreaded king then gave him an order: he was to save the suffering people of the world and prevent them from falling into hell like an endless parade of lemmings. 'If those sorry souls would make but one pilgrimage to the 33 shrines dedicated to Kannon then they would be saved,' lamented the king. Thus, he instructed Tokudo to go forth and spread the word of Kannon's mercy. When Tokudo asked for some proof to show to people, King Enma gave him 33 jewelled seals.

In the meantime, Tokudo's followers had stood vigil by his body for three days and nights and noticed that his body had not grown cold. They were astonished when their master returned to them fully healed, and with renewed vigour the group quickly set out to establish the 33 sites and propagate belief in the goddess Kannon.

The 13th stop on the Saigoku Kannon Pilgrimage route is Ishiyama Temple. According to legend, the courtesan and writer Murasaki Shikibu came to the temple in the year 1004 and prayed to Kannon, wishing for success in writing a novel. As she watched the moon reflected on the still surface of nearby Lake Biwa, the idea for *The Tale of Genji* came to her. She began writing the story in a room at the temple that is still maintained today as the 'Genji Room', complete with a life-sized figure of the author.

THE NUMBER 33 IS CONSIDERED SACRED TO KANNON, AND SHE IS BELIEVED TO HAVE 33 FORMS.

OPPOSITE: **Dating back to 747CE, Ishiyama-dera in Shiga Prefecture is the thirteenth temple on the Kansai Kannon Pilgrimage route.**

ABOVE: **A huge float of King Enma, lord of hell, is carried through the streets during the Noboribetsu Jigoku Matsuri held annually in Noboribetsu, Hokkaido.**

King Enma

Enma is the Buddhist king of the afterlife and judge of the dead who originated with the Hindu god Yama before merging with the Daoist deity Taishan Fujin in China. He wears the robes of a Chinese magistrate and a crown or hat emblazoned with the character for 'king'. Although his expression is fearsome, he is merciful and just, as we have seen in the story about the origins of the Kannon pilgrimage. He is sometimes associated with Susanowo, who also rules over the underworld, although the Shinto land of the dead, Yomi, is distinct from the Buddhist hell. While Enma is rarely directly worshipped, he frequently appears in popular culture, for example, in the characters based on him in many horror and fantasy franchises.

Jizō

Another deity of the dead, the bodhisattva Kṣitigarbha is known as Jizō in Japan. He is particularly associated with children and is guardian of the souls of *mizuko*, which are aborted, stillborn or miscarried foetuses, as well as the guardian deity of travellers. Little statues of Jizō are a common sight along roadsides and in graveyards. In graveyards, they can often be seen with bright red bibs tied around their necks, left there by parents grieving a dead child. Sometimes a pile of small stones will be placed before them, which are believed to relieve the children of their suffering in the afterlife.

Lafcadio Hearn, the 19th-century writer who introduced Japanese culture to the West, translated a *wasan* (psalm) called The Legend of the Humming of the Sai-no-Kawara. The Sai-no-Kawara is the sandy bank of the riverbed that flows at the boundary between life and death, similar to the children's limbo in Catholic theology. The psalm tells the tale of the souls of dead infants who must pray for their salvation by making towers stacked from the stones of the river's shore.

Not of this world is the story of sorrow.
The story of the Sai-no-Kawara,
At the roots of the Mountain of Shide;
Not of this world is the tale; yet 'tis most pitiful to hear.
For together in the Sai-no-Kawara are assembled
Children of tender age in multitude,
Infants but two or three years old,
Infants of four or five, infants of less than ten:

In the Sai-no-Kawara are they gathered together.
And the voice of their longing for their parents,
The voice of their crying for their mothers and their fathers
– 'Chichi koishi! Haha koishi!' –
Is never as the voice of the crying of children in this world,
But a crying so pitiful to hear
That the sound of it would pierce through flesh and bone.
And sorrowful indeed the task which they perform.
Gathering the stones of the bed of the river,
Therewith to heap the tower of prayers.
Saying prayers for the happiness of father, they heap the first tower;
Saying prayers for the happiness of mother, they heap the second
    tower;
Saying prayers for their brothers, their sisters, and all whom they
    loved at home, they heap the third tower.

RIGHT: **Jizō statues wearing red bibs stand in a line at Hida Folk Village in Gifu Prefecture.**

Such, by day, are their pitiful diversions.
But ever as the sun begins to sink below the horizon,
Then do the Oni, the demons of the hells, appear,
And say to them:

What is this that you do here?
Lo! your parents still living in the Shaba-world
Take no thought of pious offering or holy work
They do nought but mourn for you from the morning unto the evening.
Oh, how pitiful! alas! how unmerciful!
Verily the cause of the pains that you suffer
Is only the mourning, the lamentation of your parents.
And saying also, 'Blame never us!'
The demons cast down the heaped-up towers,
They dash the stones down with their clubs of iron.
But lo! the teacher Jizō appears.
All gently he comes, and says to the weeping infants:

Be not afraid, dears! be never fearful!
Poor little souls, your lives were brief indeed!
Too soon you were forced to make the weary journey to the Meido,
The long journey to the region of the dead!
Trust to me! I am your father and mother in the Meido,
Father of all children in the region of the dead.

CELEBRATED ON 3 FEBRUARY, SETSOBUN IS A CUSTOM THAT DEVELOPED DURING THE MUROMACHI PERIOD (1388–1477) AND NOW TAKES PLACE AS PART OF THE MORE GENERAL SPRING FESTIVALSTHE SEASOM BRINGS.

And he folds the skirt of his shining robe about them;
So graciously takes he pity on the infants.
To those who cannot walk he stretches forth his strong shakujō
And he pets the little ones, caresses them, takes them to his loving
bosom
So graciously he takes pity on the infants.

Namu Amida Butsu!

– translation by Lafcadio Hearn

Festival: Setsubun

Celebrated on 3 February, Setsubun is a custom that developed
during the Muromachi period (1338–1477) and now takes place as
part of the more general spring festivals the season brings.

The main ritual observed is called *mamemaki*, or bean
scattering, which can take place at home or at the workplace.

BELOW: **People perform
the** *mamemaki*, **or bean
scattering, ritual during
the spring festival of
Setsubun.**

Roasted soybeans are thrown either out of the front door or at someone wearing an *oni* mask. This ritual serves to purify the home or office by driving away evil spirits that bring misfortune.

Dōsojin

The generic name *dōsojin* refers to a type of Shinto *kami* that are the tutelary deities of borders, including those between this world and the underworld, and of paths, which help to protect travellers and pilgrims as well as those in 'transitional' states. *Dōsojin* reside within stone markers along village boundaries, mountain passes, roads and so on. The stones may be natural or carved into human forms and are sometimes enshrined within small roadside Shinto shrines known as *hokora*.

Jizō falls into the category of *dōsojin*, as does the deity Sae-no-kami. Sae-no-kami is named in the *Kojiki* as one of the children birthed during Izanagi's flight from the underworld of Yomi after looking upon the rotting corpse of his wife. Specifically, Sae-no-kami was born from a stick that he threw to stop the *oni* (evil spirits) pursuing him, and so Sae-no-kami protects the boundary between worlds by blocking the passage of the spirits of the dead into the land of the living.

Inari

Another hugely popular deity is Inari, a Shinto deity of prosperity, rice, tea, agriculture and blacksmithing , who possibly developed out of older *kami* such as the food goddesses slain by Tsukuyomi or Susano-wo. Inari can be depicted as male, female or of ambiguous gender, but is often in the company of one of its fox messengers, or *kitsune*.

A tale recounted in the *Yamashiro Fudoki*, an ancient report on the Yamashiro area, tells of how a prosperous man named Hata no Kimi Irogu made a shooting target out of a pounded sticky rice cake. When his arrow pierced the rice cake, it transformed into a white bird that flew and landed atop a mountain, where it then turned back into rice. When Irogu followed the bird's path up the mountain and found a flourishing natural rice paddy, he began worshipping the *kami* there. The name Inari comes from *ine-nari*, the Japanese words for 'rice' and 'growing'.

Inari's Buddhist association is with Kōbō Daishi, saint and founder of the Shingon sect who is also known by the name Kūkai. A Buddhist legend tells how Kōbō Daishi met a sprightly old man carrying a heavy sheaf of rice who he immediately recognized as the deity of food and plenty. After he was appointed as head priest by the emperor, Kōbō Daishi made Inari the guardian deity of Toji temple. Inari also has syncretic associations with Dakini, a *kami* we will meet later.

Rice is Japan's staple food, so it is no wonder that Inari has enjoyed such popularity. As a *kami* of prosperity and general success, Inari's concerns have shifted along with definitions of success. While originally a rural

ABOVE: **The Shinto deity Inari appears to a warrior, accompanied by a fox companion in this woodblock print by Utagawa Kuniyoshi (1798–1861).**

kami of agriculture, with the growing commercialism of the Edo period Inari became a patron of the new merchant class, and from the Meiji period (1868–1912) onwards they developed an association with industry and finance.

Thousands of shrines dedicated to Inari, both Shinto and Buddhist, can be found across Japan, identifiable by their bright red *torii* gates and fox statues. The most famous of these, and Inari's head shrine, is Fushimi Inari Grand Shrine in Kyoto with its stunning procession of *senbon torii* (1000 *torii* gates).

RAIJIN IS PORTRAYED AS A MISCHIEF MAKER WHO HAS A FIXATIONON HUMAN NAVELS. ADULTS WILL OFTEN TELL CHILDREN THAT IF THEY DON'T COVER THEIR BELLY BUTTON, THE THUNDER GOD WILL COME AND SNATCH IT AWAY.

As a deity of food, it is only fitting that Inari has several dishes named after them. One of these is *inari-zushi*, a popular type of sushi that consists of a rice ball wrapped in sweet, deep-fried tofu. A common addition to a boxed lunch or sushi platter, they are also left as offerings for the *kitsune* messengers at Inari shrines.

Fūjin & Raijin

As deities named in the *Kojiki*, Fūjin and his brother Raijin are among the oldest of the gods. Fūjin is the *kami* of the wind, whereas Raijin rules over thunder, lightning and storms. The brothers were born from the rotting corpse of Izanagi in the underworld and escaped into the human world as Izanami fled from her hideous form. They were some of the demons tasked with killing humans as Izanami's revenge on Izanagi. However, while these destructive *kami* can wreak havoc, they can also benefit humankind; after all, storms bring rain that waters the crops.

RIGHT: **Fūjin, the god of wind, is depicted on the left side of this decorative folding screen by Kōrin Ogata (1658–1716).**

Fūjin is commonly shown as a ferocious blue or green demon with horns and fangs who grasps the ends of a sack from which the wind blows forth. The possession of this wind bag has been used as evidence by some historians to trace Fūjin's origins back along the Silk Road to the Chinese wind deity Feng Bo, from there to the north Indian Greco-Buddhist Oado, and eventually back to the Greek god Boreas. Similarities can be seen in the visual depictions of all these deities.

Raijin is an equally fearsome deity who is pictured standing above a cloud and beating on *den-den daiko* drums, his hair rising up threateningly from his head. In a more humorous side to him, Raijin is portrayed as a mischief maker who has a fixation on human navels. Adults will often tell children that if they don't cover their belly button, the Thunder God will come and snatch it away.

Although the brothers are seen as powerfully destructive forces, these powers are not always used against humanity; they

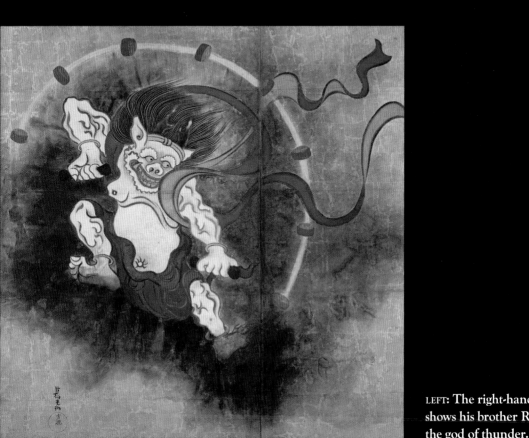

LEFT: **The right-hand fold shows his brother Raijin, the god of thunder.**

ABOVE: **Women perform a dance called the *Bon Odori* during the summer festival held to honour deceased ancestors.**

can also act as protectors. In 1274 the Mongols attempted to invade Japan, but their efforts were thwarted by a great storm. When a second invasion was attempted in 1281, another typhoon swept through and obliterated the fleet. While it is not clear which deity supposedly sent the storms, it is generally attributed to Raijin, Ryūjin, Hachiman or all three. These two storms were named *kamikaze* or 'divine wind', a phrase that would see a resurgence during World War II.

Sculptures of Fūjin and Raijin stand guard at Asakusa on either side of the famous outer gate to Senso-ji, known as Kaminarimon or the 'Thunder Gate', to protect the temple from wind and storms.

Festival: Obon

The Japanese festival of Obon originated from the Chinese Ghost Festival and has been celebrated in Japan for over 500 years. It is a time of year when spirits of the dead return briefly to the land of the living. A Buddhist story tells of how Mokuren, a disciple of the Buddha, used his supernatural powers to view his deceased mother and saw that her spirit had fallen into the Realm of Hungry Ghosts and was suffering greatly. When Mokuren asked the Buddha how he could save his mother, the Buddha told him to make offerings to Buddhist monks on the fifteenth day of the seventh month. This he did, and his mother was released from suffering. Mokuren danced with joy, thinking of the kindness his mother had always shown him and the sacrifices she had made for him during her life.

Traditionally, a dance called the *Bon Odori* is performed during the festival to welcome the spirits of the dead. The festival's dance and music varies significantly between regions, from the *Sōran Bushi* in Hokkaidō to the *Awa Odori* in Shikoku. Today, the religious aspects of the festival have faded, and the street dancing serves more as entertainment. Still, many families engage in customs that honour their ancestors, such as visiting the graves of departed family members and placing offerings to welcome the arrival of their ancestors.

Originally a Buddhist-Confucian custom, Obon is now observed more generally as a time for families to come together in celebration and remembrance. As it is held during the hot Japanese summer, many attendees wear *yukata*, a kind of light cotton kimono, and enjoy summer street food such as *kakigōri*, a dessert of shaved ice covered in flavoured syrup. Obon and other summer festivals evoke a strong sense of nostalgia and bittersweet reflection, and hot summer nights are also a traditional time for telling ghost stories.

The Empress Jingū

Empress Jingū is one of only a handful of women who have reigned on the Chrysanthemum Throne. A reigning empress is called the empress regnant whereas the wife of an emperor is the empress consort. One day, while she was still empress consort, Jingū received a vision from Watatsumi, the god of the sea, commanding her husband, Emperor Chuai, to take an army across the ocean to invade lands to the west. When she told him this, Chuai dismissed it. Angered, Watatsumi told the

THE JAPANESE FESTIVAL OF OBON ORIGINATED FROM THE CHINESE GHOST FESTIVAL AND HAS BEEN CELEBRATED IN JAPAN FOR OVER 500 YEARS.

emperor, 'You shall not rule this promised land,' and not long after, Chuai died.

Jingū became empress regent and soon set about fulfilling the gods' wishes. However, there was one small problem – she was pregnant by her late husband. Not to be deterred, she tied heavy rocks around her waist and was able to delay the birth for the three years it took to successfully conquer the lands with her armies. As soon as she arrived back in Japan, she gave birth to a baby boy.

Empress Jingū and her son Ojin are the last of the 'legendary' emperors recorded in the *Kojiki* and *Nihon Shoki*, before the later 'semi-legendary' emperors for whom some historical evidence exists. Although modern scholars consider them to be completely fantastical figures without a basis in real history, they have not always been considered as such. The Meiji government's promotion of State Shinto from the 1870s meant that Jingū and her forebears were regarded as historical fact, and Jingū's overseas expansion efforts were celebrated. The 'promised land' she sought was often interpreted as referring to the Korean Peninsula, and this was partly used to justify Japan's annexation of Korea in 1910 and the subsequent regime, despite the lack of proof that any past invasions had ever occurred. After the end of the war, Empress Jingū fell from favour due to her associations with Japan's nationalistic foreign policy, and scholarship around her remains mired in controversy.

Sumiyoshi Grand Shrine in Osaka was founded in the 11th year of Empress Jingū's reign by a powerful local family. When she visited, Empress Jingū told the head priest to enshrine the *Sumiyoshi sanjin*, three Shinto deities of the sea and sailing. The empress herself was later enshrined there, too. The shrine makes an appearance in *The Tale of Genji* and is also the shrine where the old couple in the tale of Issun-bōshi prayed for a child.

Hachiman

Hachiman, whose name translates as 'eight banners', is a god of war as well as of culture and learning. As the divine protector of Japan and the imperial household, he is the god who, depending on the version, either sent the thunder and wind gods to detonate the *kamikaze* against the Mongols or conjured up the divine winds himself.

Shinto beliefs state that Hachiman is the deification of the legendary Emperor Ojin, son of Empress Jingū, whose mythological birth and reign are recorded in the *Kojiki* and the *Nihon Shoki*. Emperor Ojin had many wives and children, but he still had time to cement his reputation as a man of culture who was open to ideas and literature from China and Korea and saw to it that the people of his court were educated.

Hachiman seems to have been worshipped as a popular god from at least the Nara period (710–794), but saw his popularity grow during the chaos of the Genpei War when he became closely associated with the first shogun Minamoto Yoritomo and his son, Minamoto Yoriie. He enjoyed another resurgence during the Edo period as patron of the warrior class of samurai and then again after the Meiji Restoration and during World War II.

Hachiman's shrines are known as *Hachimangū* and can be found throughout Japan, the central and most famous being Usa Shrine in Ōita Prefecture. The earliest recorded use of a *mikoshi*

OPPOSITE: **A hanging scroll featuring the legendary Empress Jingū by famous woodblock artist Katsushika Hokusai (1615–1868).**

portable shrine was in 749 when one was used to carry the spirit
of Hachiman from Usa to Kyoto to watch over the construction
of the *Daibutsu* giant Buddha at Tōdai-ji.

The Sea God

The deity of the sea is often referred to either as Watatsumi or
Ryūjin, the Dragon King; although they were originally two
separate deities, they became fused at some point and are now
generally seen as interchangeable. Watatsumi is named as one
of the children of Izanagi and Izanami in the *Kojiki*. The god of
the sea takes the form of a dragon, a mythical creature closely
associated with water, and lives in the Ryūgū-jō, a palace beneath
the waves.

The sea god plays a part in various tales including the tale
of Hoderi and Hoori and the story of Empress Jingū, as well as
having encounters with legendary heroes such as Tawara Toda
and Urashima Tarō.

As an island nation that relied on the oceans surrounding
it for food as well as trade, the sea features heavily in Japanese
mythology. Shrines to Watatsumi or Ryūjin can be found
throughout the country, particularly in rural and coastal areas.

Dakiniten

In Hinduism and Buddhism, the *ḍādkinī* were demonesses, but through Kūkai's introduction of esoteric Shingon Buddhism to Japan in the early Heian period (794–1192), they coalesced into a deity known as Dakiniten or Dakini who eventually came to be seen as the Buddhist manifestation of the Shinto deity Inari, likely due to their common association with foxes. She is often shown as a semi-nude woman riding a white fox and carrying a wish-fulfilling jewel.

Dakiniten is seen as a wish-fulfiller, and the success of certain legendary heroes has been attributed to her. A story from *Genpei Seisuiki*, an extended version of the *Heiki Monogatari* that encompasses 48 books, tells a tale of Taira no Kiyomori's encounter with Dakiniten.

One day, when Kiyomori was out hunting, he shot a fox only for it to transform into a beautiful woman. The woman said that she was a servant of Dakiniten, and in return for not killing her, she would grant all his desires. Kiyomori spared the fox-woman's life and began to worship Dakini. Soon after, his family grew prosperous and powerful, and the Taira were, for a time, the most powerful clan in the land.

Dakiniten is the guardian deity of Myōgon-ji in Aichi Prefecture. The Shinto Buddhist fusion is clear here with the popular name for the temple being Toyokawa Inari, and the entrance featuring a red *torii* gate despite it technically being a Zen Buddhist temple.

HOW THE JELLYFISH LOST ITS BONES

Published in English as a children's fairytale, this story is one of many featuring the Dragon King. However, despite featuring in a book of translations, the Japanese origins of the story are rather obscure; it may well be more a product of the translator's own imagination. Still, this simply continues the time-honoured tradition by which deities evolved and changed during their journeys through India, Tibet, China, Japan, and now the West.

The story goes that one day, in his glittering palace under the sea, Ryūjin the Dragon King decided that he wanted a monkey's liver; whether as a medicine or simply on a whim depends on the version.

Ryūjin was the lord of all sea creatures, from fish to sea turtles, and on this day he summoned the jellyfish to do his bidding. The jellyfish was concerned that he had neither the strength nor the dexterity to capture a creature of the land, and so he set out to use his words and cunning. To lure the monkey down from the trees, he spoke of the beauty of the underwater palace and its walls of pink coral and floors of shining mother of pearl. Entranced, the monkey scampered down the tree trunks, but as they began talking, the jellyfish, feeling bad for the monkey, let slip the true purpose of his visit. Thinking on his feet, the monkey told the jellyfish that he had a spare liver up in the trees, he just had to go and get it; but of course, as soon as he was up in the treetops, he disappeared.

Ashamed, the jellyfish returned to Ryūjin to report his failure. Back beneath the waves, Dragon King was so angry that he crushed the jellyfish flat, and from that day onwards, all the jellyfish's descendants were soft and boneless.

A statue of Ryūjin, the Dragon King of the sea.

Festival: Niiname-no-Matsuri

The Niiname-no-Matsuri is a harvest ritual that is officially celebrated by the emperor of Japan on 23 November when he thanks the Shinto deities for the bounty of the previous year and prays for a fruitful harvest in the coming year. The festival was briefly abolished after World War II when occupying US forces sought to stamp out any holidays rooted in Shinto mythology, but a secular holiday, Labour Thanksgiving Day, was instead instituted on the same date.

In 2014, Prince Naruhito composed a *waka* poem in which he appreciates the sound of the sacred *Mikagura* music performed outside as heard within the silence of the Sanctuary as he accompanied the emperor at the *Niiname-sai* ceremony in Imperial Palace: '*The graceful sound of singing is heard in the stillness of the Sanctuary during the Niiname-sa*'.

Himiko

According to *Records of the Three Kingdoms*, a Chinese chronicle dating from the 3rd century, a shamaness queen named Himiko ruled over the kingdom of Yamatai in the land of Wa (Japan) during the Yayoi period (c.300BCE–c.250CE). However, despite mentions in historical documents from both China and Korea, no note of Himiko is made in either the *Kojiki* or the *Nihon Shoki*, and there is much debate over her actual existence and the location of Yamatai. Some scholars maintain that the megalithic tomb of Hashihaka kofun in Nara Prefecture, which is associated with the emergence of the Yamato dynasty, is the tomb of Himiko, although this has not been proved. In fact, the mythological legacy of

BELOW: **A regal statue of Himiko, Queen of Yamatai, stands at the north exit of Kanzaki railway station in Saga Prefecture.**

Queen Himiko of Yamatai is relatively modern, with interest in her growing during the Edo period. Standing outside the official mythological corpus, she is a mysterious figure that some people wish to keep apart from but who others seek to integrate into the official imperial lineage.

Himiko is often reinterpreted in popular culture as a beautiful, sensual sorceress. Her name has been given to a Lyman-alpha blob, a massive concentration of hydrogen gas believed to be a protogalaxy, which was discovered in 2009.

Ōtoshi

Also known as Toshigami, Ōtoshi is a Shinto *kami* who is the son of Susano-wo and older brother to Inari. He is himself the father of many other deities with his several wives. He is thought to be an amalgamation of folk deities that protect the rice fields and the harvest as well as watching over the ancestral spirits known as *sorei*. He is now considered to be the 'god of the year' who helps to usher in the new year.

Festival: Oshōgatsu

Since 1873, the Japanese New Year has been celebrated on 1 January, in line with the Gregorian calendar. Families gather at their *jikka*, or main household, to celebrate the passing of one

RIGHT: **To celebrate New Year's Day, many households eat a traditional meal called** *osechi-ryōri.*

year into the next. There are many special foods eaten at this time of year, for example, a dish called *osechi-ryōri*. Another is *toshikoshi-soba*, or year-crossing soba noodles, which is specifically eaten on Ōmisoka, or New Year's Eve. Mochi, or pounded rice cakes, are another staple; pounding sticky white rice into mochi with a large wooden mallet is a common tradition. Either at midnight, or over the following days, people visit the local shrine in a custom called *hatsumōde*, the first shrine visit of the new year.

Tenjin

Tenjin is another example of a *hitogami* – a human who is worshipped as a deity. Sugawara Michizane was a brilliant and accomplished scholar in the Heian court. However, at the beginning of the 10th century, he was set up by the rivals of the imperial court and falsely accused of treason, after which he was exiled from the capital and died soon after. Following this, the capital was struck by plague, famine and tremendous storms that caused great damage. Sugawara then appeared to the emperor as a *goryō*, or angry spirit. To placate the spirit, the emperor reinstated Sugawara's offices and withdrew the order of exile. Finally, when he deified the scholar as a *kami* named Tenjin, the troubles plaguing the capital ceased.

At first, as a god of natural disasters, Tenjin was worshipped to avoid his curses. However, as a famed poet during his lifetime, from the Edo period onwards scholars began to see him as a patron of scholarship and learning. Today, many students and their parents pray to his shrines before school and university entrance exams and offer thanks for their successes afterwards.

ABOVE: **A painting by Nagasawa Rosetsu (1754–1799) shows the Heian scholar Sugawara Michizane in his deified form of Tenjin.**

Shrines dedicated to Sugawara and his deified form as Tenjin are called *Tenmangū*. Dazaifu Tenmangū is one of the head shrines that is built over Sugawara's grave. During his exile, Sugawara composed a famous poem about his love of the capital's plum trees, and legend has it that the plum trees growing at the shrine flew from Kyoto to be with him in death. Another tale tells of how his body was carried by an ox to his burial site, where there now stands a statue of an ox to commemorate this.

Dainichi Nyorai

Dainichi Nyorai is the central deity of Esoteric Buddhism, a form of the religion that emphasizes mysticism and austere ritual practice. Followers believe that through personal worship of a deity, they may gain insight into secret teachings, and by following them reach enlightenment. It flourished in Japan in the Heian period after a Buddhist monk named Kūkai founded the Shingon sect following his travels in China.

'Dainichi' means 'great sun', and 'Nyorai' is a synonym for 'Buddha'. As he is the supreme sun Buddha, followers consider the Shinto deity Amaterasu to be a manifestation of Dainichi. Dainichi Nyorai is pictured as a man dressed in the fashion of the nobility of ancient India seated atop a lotus petal and surrounded by a halo representing the light emitted by the Buddha. A wooden statue of him sculpted

in 1176 by the famous sculptor Unkei sits at Enjō-ji, a Shingon temple in Nara Prefecture.

Fudō Myōō

The deity Acala was not a major deity in Indian or Tibetan Buddhism, but as Fudō Myōō he became central to the Shingon Buddhist esoteric sect in Japan. Many prominent priests, including Kūkai, the founder of the Shingon school, worshipped Fudō Myōō, and he was seen as a guardian of ritual practitioners as well as a protector of the imperial court and entire nation. Yamabushi mountain ascetics will often pray to small Fudō Myōō talismen when engaging in Shugendō, a form of ascetic training in the mountains.

Fudō Myōō is a wrathful deity who represents the power of Buddhism to overcome earthly passions and protect the faith from its enemies. The name Fudō means 'immovable' and as a messenger of Dainichi Nyorai he carries his wrath against evil and ignorance. He is often depicted standing straight-backed on firmly planted legs with a sword used to slice through ignorance and a lasso to reign in anyone who blocks the path to enlightenment. His face is ferocious and threatening to subdue evil and frighten non-believers.

ABOVE: **Tsukioka Yoshitoshi (1839–1892) illustrates a legend in which Fudō Myōō threatens a novice who wants to become a wise monk.**

OPPOSITE: **Wooden sculpture of Dainichi Nyorai, the Supreme Buddha in Esoteric Buddhism, from the Heian period.**

THE STORY
GOES THAT
TAKEMINAKATA
DEFEATED MORIYA
USING ONLY A
WISTERIA VINE.

Takeminakata

Also known as Suwa Myōjin, this *kami* is the deity of Lake
Suwa and Suwa Grand Shrine in Nagano Prefecture and a son
of Ōkuninushi. He was worshipped as a god of wind, water and
agriculture, as well as hunting and warfare, which made him
popular with samurai clans during the medieval period. He is the
mythical ancestor of the Suwa clan, and the high priests of the
Suwa Grand Shrine were regarded as his living vessels.

There are many local legends about him and Moriya, a local
kami who Takeminakata fought when he first arrived at Lake
Suwa. The story goes that Takeminakata defeated Moriya using
only a wisteria vine. Some historians regard these stories as
mythologized versions of a historical conflict between an original
local clan and a group of invaders who went on to become the
Suwa clan, a family of powerful priests and later samurai.

Shichi Fukujin: The Seven Lucky Gods

These seven gods of fortune are believed to represent good luck
and often feature as little carved *netsuke* figures in shops or
homes. All of them represent *kami* of wealth and happiness in
some form, and this disparate group have emerged from Buddhist,
Daoist and native Shinto origins to form a diverse and somewhat
ragtag crew. The *Takarabune* ('Treasure Ship') is a mythical ship
that sails through the heavens during the first three days of the
new year carrying the seven lucky gods and bringing them to
ports in the human world. During the Muromachi period it was
popular to place a woodblock print of the *Takarabune* under one's
pillow on the night of 2 January to induce a lucky dream and
good fortune in the coming year.

Ebisu

Ebisu is a native Japanese god, and the *kami* of luck, commerce
and fishermen. He started to be worshipped during the late Heian
period and is usually depicted wearing Heian-era clothing and a
tall, brimless black hat. He has a jolly expression and carries a
large red sea bream in one hand and often a fishing rod in the
other. As a patron of good fortune, Ebisu is very popular and his
figure is commonly found in fish restaurants.

Ebisu is rather an enigmatic *kami*; although there is no mention of him in the chronicles, he has become associated with Hiruko the Leech Child and Kotoshironushi. After the Leech Child was born limbless to Izanagi and Izanami, they set him adrift in a reed basket. He eventually washed ashore and as he overcame the hardships of life on land, he grew legs. In spite of being slightly disabled and deaf, he is always in good humour. Being deaf, he does not hear the summons to the *kami's* annual meeting, and so is still around during the *Kannazuki* month without gods.

There are many shrines dedicated to Ebisu, the main one being Nishinomiya Shrine in Hyōgo Prefecture, which is also known as Ebessan. Yebisu Beer, now brewed by Sapporo Brewery, takes its name from the *kami* and features his likeness on the can. The Ebisu area of Shibuya in Tokyo originally developed around the brewing company, and there is a cheerful statue of the *kami* in front of the station.

BELOW: **The Seven Lucky Gods, or Shichi Fukujin, sit in a circle. Unknown artist circa 1878.**

Daikokuten

This powerful god has his origins in Mahākāla, the Buddhist version of the Hindu deity Shiva, giving him an identification with darkness and magic. After his arrival in Japan through esoteric Buddhist sects, he became syncretically associated with the Shinto *kami* Ōkuninushi. As Ōkuninushi is the earth god, Daikokuten is seen as a protector of luck and wealth that derives from the earth. He is generally portrayed as a fat, jolly man sitting atop bales of rice and carrying a mallet. Whenever he bashes the mallet, it releases a shower of gold coins. He is sometimes accompanied by rats and mice. Especially important to farmers and merchants, he is seen as Ebisu's father and is often enshrined together with his son in shop shrines or in the kitchen.

ABOVE: **A red snapper dreams about Ebisu using an abacus, by Toyohiro Utagawa (1773–1828).**

OPPOSITE: **Benzaiten is surrounded by fifteen attendants in this hanging scroll from the Kamakura period by an unknown artist.**

Bishamonten

Connected to the Hindu god Kubera, Bishamonten is a god of fortune in war and is shown dressed in Chinese-style armour, carrying a halberd in one hand and a mini pagoda in the other. A traditional pagoda was a reliquary used to store Buddhist scrolls, and as such Bishamonten is the protector of Buddhist law and of all those who follow the rules and show integrity. He is also a member of the Shitenno, the Buddhist Four Heavenly Kings where he goes by the name Tamonten.

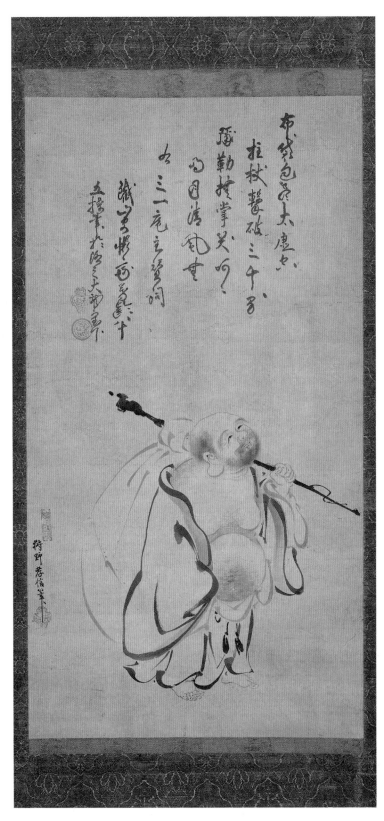

Benzaiten

The only female of the group, Benzaiten (or simply Benten) stems from the Hindu goddess Saraswati and came to Japan through classical Chinese translations of the Golden Light Sutra. Syncretically, she is associated with Ugajin, a Shinto *kami* of fertility with the body of a snake and a human head. She is a goddess of beauty, music and talent as well as a patron of artists, writers, dancers and geisha.

Benzaiten is depicted as a beautiful woman in luxurious medieval Chinese robes who carries a *biwa*, a traditional instrument similar to a lute. She may also have a snake on her head, either with or without a human face, due to the association with Ugajin.

Shrine pavilions dedicated to Benzaiten are called *bentendō*. These are often situated beside a body of water as she is also identified as a water deity. Along with many others, she is enshrined at the Three Great Benzaiten Shrines at Enoshima in Sagami Bay, Chikubu Island in Lake Biwa and Itsukushima Island in

Ryukyuan *Kang*

The Ryukyuan call their deities *kang*. They are powerful beings who are depicted in Chinese clothing like that of the Okinawan nobility. They enter the human world through sacred groves and caves. They are generally neutral so long as people carry out the appropriate rituals and behave correctly, but they do have the power to interfere in human lives when this is not the case.

There are several categories of *kang*, although these definitions are nebulous. There are the heavenly *ting nu kang*, including the *kangs* of the sea, water and sun. Then there are the many local *kang* as well as *kang* for various occupations. The ancestors are called *futuki* and they can be called upon to mediate between the living and the *kang*.

the Seto Inland Sea. Itsukushima Shrine is built over the water and is famous for its 'floating' *torii* gate.

Zeniarai Benzaiten Ugafuku Shrine in Kanagawa Prefecture is dedicated to a Shinto–Buddhist fusion of the *kami* Ugajin and the goddess Benzaiten. It is popular thanks to a myth that washing money in the waters of the spring that flows there will multiply it, and visitors still flock to the shrine today to wash coins and notes.

Jurojin

Jurojin is a personification of the southern pole star from Chinese Daoisim. He may be based on a real historical figure, possibly a Daoist sage from ancient China. A god of longevity and the elderly, he has an elongated head and a long beard and is often accompanied by a deer, a crane or a tortoise, all symbols of long life. He leans on a cane and has a scroll or book with him that contains the secrets of life.

Although often depicted with a serious expression, Jurojin loves to drink and make merry. He is a popular subject of Japanese ink wash paintings, with artists from the Muromachi period onwards depicting his likeness in delicate brush strokes.

Hotei (Budai)

Another former human, Hotei is a deified priest of Chinese Zen Buddhism. Known as Budai in China, he is a later addition

OPPOSITE: Hotei illustrated in ink by Kanō Takanobu (1571–1618) with calligraphy by Tetsuzan Sōdon.

AINU *KAMUY*

The Ainu people's gods are called *kamuy*, and their stories have been passed down orally and through ritual traditions. Like *kami*, they are spiritual beings that can include animals, plants, weather or objects. There are good *pirika kamuy*, hostile *wen kamuy* and neutral *kamuy* called *koshne*.

Humans and *kamuy* share a reciprocal relationship, with humans providing offerings of food, wine, song and dance to the deities. These offerings are facilitated by an *inau*, a stick with carefully shaved curling strips at the end. *Kamuy* would come to the Ainu homeland 'dressed' in the guise of plants or animals, a disguise called a *hayopke*, and would then leave these behind imbued with their *ramat* (spirit) as gifts for the Ainu people after being given a proper ritual send-off.

The most important named *kamuy* to the Ainu is *Kamuy-huci*, the goddess of the hearth. She serves as the gateway between the human world and the *kamuy*, and it is through her that all prayers need to pass. She is the guardian of the home and lives in the hearth, whose fire must never be extinguished.

to the Japanese pantheon, who made his way over with the establishment of Zen Buddhism in the 13th century, although it was during the Edo period that his popularity surged.

He is a wanderer who dresses simply with a shirt that doesn't fasten over his protruding stomach. The bulging sack he carries with him represents the luck and gifts he readily gives to his patrons, particularly children. His likeness is familiar in the Western world as the Laughing Buddha, a fat, jovial little man with a big belly and long earlobes – this image is often conflated with the Buddha himself, although this is a misconception.

Fukurokuju

Another god of Chinese origin, his roots most likely lie in a mythical hermit from the Song dynasty who was also said to be a manifestation of the south polar star. He is a god of wisdom, longevity and sometimes carnal pleasure. He is depicted as a small, dwarf-like man in Chinese clothes with a bald head fringed by a ring of hair.

Fukurokuju's spot in the Lucky Seven was originally taken by Kichijoten, but now he is generally considered to be an established member. However, he is sometimes combined with Jurojin due to having a similar origin as one of the Three Star Gods.

Kichijoten

Probably the most elusive and obscure of all the Lucky Seven, Kichijoten is a female deity adapted via Buddhism from the Hindu goddess Lakshmi who sometimes replaces Fukurokuju in the Seven. She is often depicted as a noblewoman, and is a goddess of happiness, fortune, beauty and the feminine; as such, she is generally perceived as a deity worshipped by women. She is associated with the Kagome, an ancient Shinto symbol of a six-pointed star.

LEFT: **Ainu people performing a traditional dance to send the spirit of the bear back to its home.**

3

HEROES AND LEGENDS

From legendary emperors to loyal samurai and brave warriors, from tiny Tom Thumb-sized boys to ferocious demons, heroic tales have entertained the Japanese people and influenced the country's culture for centuries. Japan also has a long and rich literary and artistic tradition when it comes to recording and disseminating these tales.

Myths and storytelling

Myths and legends are inextricably linked with storytelling and literature. As mentioned previously, the *Kojiki* and *Nihon Shoki*, although written at the time as 'official' histories, can now be read as creation stories. Beyond these are a plethora of other narrative forms, including both prose and poetry, some of which we will look at in this chapter.

Monogatari

The literary tradition of *monogatari*, which literally translates as 'story', is a form of extended narrative prose, similar to the 'epic'

OPPOSITE: One of a set of woodblock prints by artists Kunisada Utagawa (1786–1864) and Kunichika Toyohara (1835–1900) which show kabuki actors performing the role of one of the forty-seven rōnin.

ABOVE: **This painting by Harunobu Gakutei (1813–1868) depicts Murasaki Shikibu composing the Tale of Genji at Ishiyamadera.**

of Western literary tradition. They were often written records of oral tales, and followed fictional stories and characters based on real people and set among real historical events. The two most famous *monogatari* are the *Genji Monogatari*, and the *Heiki Monogatari*.

The Tale of Genji

Considered to be the world's first novel in the modern sense of the word, *The Tale of Genji* was written in the early 11th-century Heian period (794–1192) by the noblewoman Murasaki Shikibu. The epic tale of aristocratic court romance follows the life of fictional character Hikaru Genji. This heroic protagonist is thought to have been inspired by the then-leader of the Fujiwara clan, Fujiwara no Michinaga. Although fictional, the novel is a valuable resource both as an insight into Heian court life and as a defining text in Japanese literature.

Genji the Shining One... He knew that the bearer of such a name could not escape much scrutiny and jealous censure and that his lightest dallyings would be proclaimed to posterity. Fearing then lest he should appear to after ages as a mere good-for-nothing and trifler, and knowing that (so accursed is the blabbing of gossips' tongues) his most secret acts might come to light, he was obliged always to act with great prudence and to preserve at least the outward appearance of respectability. Thus nothing really romantic ever happened to him and Katano no Shōshō would have scoffed at his story.

– translation by Arthur Waley

LEFT: **A painting of the scene where Hikaru Genji first glimpses the character of Murasaki while visiting Kitayama, by Tosa Mitsuoki (1617–1691).**

The Tale of the Heike

This work falls under the category of *gunki monogatari*, or stories of war and military chronicles. It is an epic account of the Genpei War, the epic struggle between the Taira and Minamoto clans for control of Japan in the early 12th century. Its authorship is indeterminate; it would have been passed down orally before ever being written down.

> '*The sound of the bell of Gionshoja echoes the impermanence of all things. The hue of the flowers of the teak tree declares that they who flourish must be brought low. Yea, the proud ones are but for a moment, like an evening dream in springtime.*'
> – translation by A. L. Sadler

The Bamboo Cutter and the Moon Maiden

While the date of its composition is unknown, *The Tale of the Bamboo Cutter* is thought to have been written in the late 9th century and is considered to be the oldest example of *monogatari*. It is also sometimes regarded as the world's oldest science fiction story, with Princess Kaguya and the Moonfolk representing extraterrestrials and the cloud on which they travelled to Earth illustrated as a flying saucer-shaped object.

One day, an old bamboo cutter was out working in the forest when he came across a stalk of bamboo that shone with a mysterious light. When he split it open, he was startled to find a tiny child inside, so small that she could fit within the palm of his hand. He took the child home with him and he and his wife, having no children of their own, agreed to raise the girl together. They named her Nayotake no Kaguya-hime, which means 'Shining Princess of the Young Bamboo'. From that day forth, whenever the old man cut down a stalk of bamboo, he found gold hiding inside. The family, once dirt poor, were suddenly rich.

Within three months, the tiny child grew into an adult woman, and a stunningly beautiful one at that. Although her adoptive parents sought to keep her hidden away, news of her beauty spread, and she was soon besieged by legions of hopeful suitors. Among them were five noblemen, who beseeched the old man to bestow his daughter upon one of their number. The

THE TALE OF THE BAMBOO CUTTER... IS SOMETIMES REGARDED AS THE WORLD'S OLDEST SCIENCE FICTION STORY.

OPPOSITE: **The princess Kaguya is found in a bamboo stalk by a lowly bamboo cutter.**

bamboo cutter informed them that as Princess Kaguya was not his daughter by blood, he did not have the authority to force her into a marriage. However, as the suitors persisted, he went to his daughter and suggested that she choose a suitable match.

Princess Kaguya responded that she would not marry a man of whose faith she could not be certain. She therefore devised five impossible tasks and agreed to marry whoever proved himself worthy by completing his task.

The Five Impossible Tasks

Of the first noble, she asked for the stone begging bowl of the Buddha himself, located in India. The noble, thinking the distance too great and the task futile, instead delivered a counterfeit to Princess Kaguya. The princess, however, saw that the bowl he presented did not glow with holy light and was not fooled.

Of the second noble, she asked for a jewelled branch from the mountain of Horai. Like his predecessor, this noble concluded that creating a fake would be the best option, and he had the finest craftspeople in the land work on it in secret. When he delivered the branch to Princess Kaguya, the noble regaled her with elaborate and false tales of his perilous quest to retrieve the branch. His lies may well have worked were it not for the arrival of the craftspeople, demanding payment for their work.

Of the third noble, she asked for flame-proof fur robes made from the pelt of the Chinese fire rat. The noble commissioned a merchant who sailed across the sea and returned with a sea-green fur robe with hairs tipped in shimmering gold. Yet when Princess Kaguya threw the furs into the fire to test it, they burned away to ash.

Of the fourth noble, she asked for a rainbow jewel found in a dragon's head. First the noble sent his men to procure the jewel, but when he learned that they had absconded, he set out across the sea himself. There he encountered a great storm and suffered terrible seasickness, and he returned to land defeated.

Of the fifth noble, she asked for a cowrie shell brought over the seas by a swallow. The noble attempted to retrieve this shell, but upon climbing to a great height to reach into the swallow's nest, he slipped and fell to his doom.

OPPOSITE: **Princess Kaguya returns to the Moon with a retinue of Moonfolk. The classic tale is sometimes regarded as proto-science fiction.**

The Moonfolk

By now, tales of Princess Kaguya had reached the imperial court, and the emperor himself asked for Princess Kaguya's hand in marriage. However, she even turned down the emperor's advances, although the pair remained in friendly written communication.

During the spring and summer of that year, Princess Kaguya descended into melancholy. She often sat awake at night, gazing up at the full Moon with tears in her eyes. Her adoptive parents grew very worried about her, until eventually she revealed the truth to them – she was no earthly woman, but a maiden of the Moon. That shining orb in the sky above was her true birthplace, and the time was soon approaching when her people would come to return her to her rightful home.

The bamboo cutter was, of course, distraught to hear this. As the date approached, the emperor sent a retinue of guards to protect the princess, even though she insisted it would be futile. Then, on the appointed night, the Moonfolk came. They descended from the heavens upon a cloud, and they shone with a strange and brilliant light. When the emperor's men fired their arrows at the Moonfolk, none landed. so the retinue arrived, and called forth the Princess Kaguya.

Knowing that she could not disobey the summons, Princess Kaguya prepared to leave. She gave her silken robe as a memento to her parents and wrote a mournful letter to the emperor, sending with it a drop of the elixir of life. After she was done, the Moonfolk put a celestial robe of feathers around her shoulders, upon which the princess immediately forgot all about her time on Earth. She stepped atop the cloud with the host of Moonfolk, and it quickly rose until it was lost to sight.

When the emperor received the princess' letter and gift, he asked his councillors, 'Of all the mountains in this land, which stands closest to the heavens?' It was suggested that a peak in Suruga Province was the highest, and so the emperor bid his men to take the letter to the top of the mountain and burn it, so that the message might reach Princess Kaguya on the Moon, and to also burn the elixir of life, for he could not bear to live for an eternity without her. According to legend, the name we now

SHE WAS NO EARTHLY WOMAN, BUT A MAIDEN OF THE MOON. THAT SHINING ORB IN THE SKY ABOVE WAS HER TRUE BIRTHPLACE.

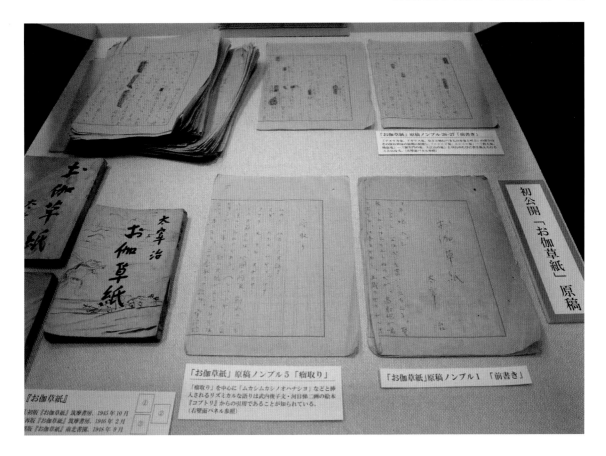

know that mountain by, Mount Fuji, came from the word *fushi*, meaning 'undying', and that the smoke from the burning letter still rises heavenward to this day.

Otogi-zōshi

The aristocratic Muromachi period (1338–1477) ushered in a new interest in folktales. The defining literary work of this medieval era is the *otogi-zōshi*, a collection of around 350 illustrated narratives. The tales range from fairy tales to accounts of the heroic exploits of real historical figures, and come from an array of often uncredited sources including aristocrats, monks, and samurai. While *monogatari* of the earlier periods were generally written by and for the aristocracy, this new genre opened up written literature and legend to a much wider and more diverse audience.

During the Taisho (1912–26) and early Shōwa (1926–45) periods, the imperial government created a series of standardized

ABOVE: **The manuscript of *otogi-zōshi* written by Japanese author Osamu Dazai (1909–48) is displayed during an exhibition at the Museum of Modern Japanese Literature in 2019. Dazai retold many of the stories in his own collection.**

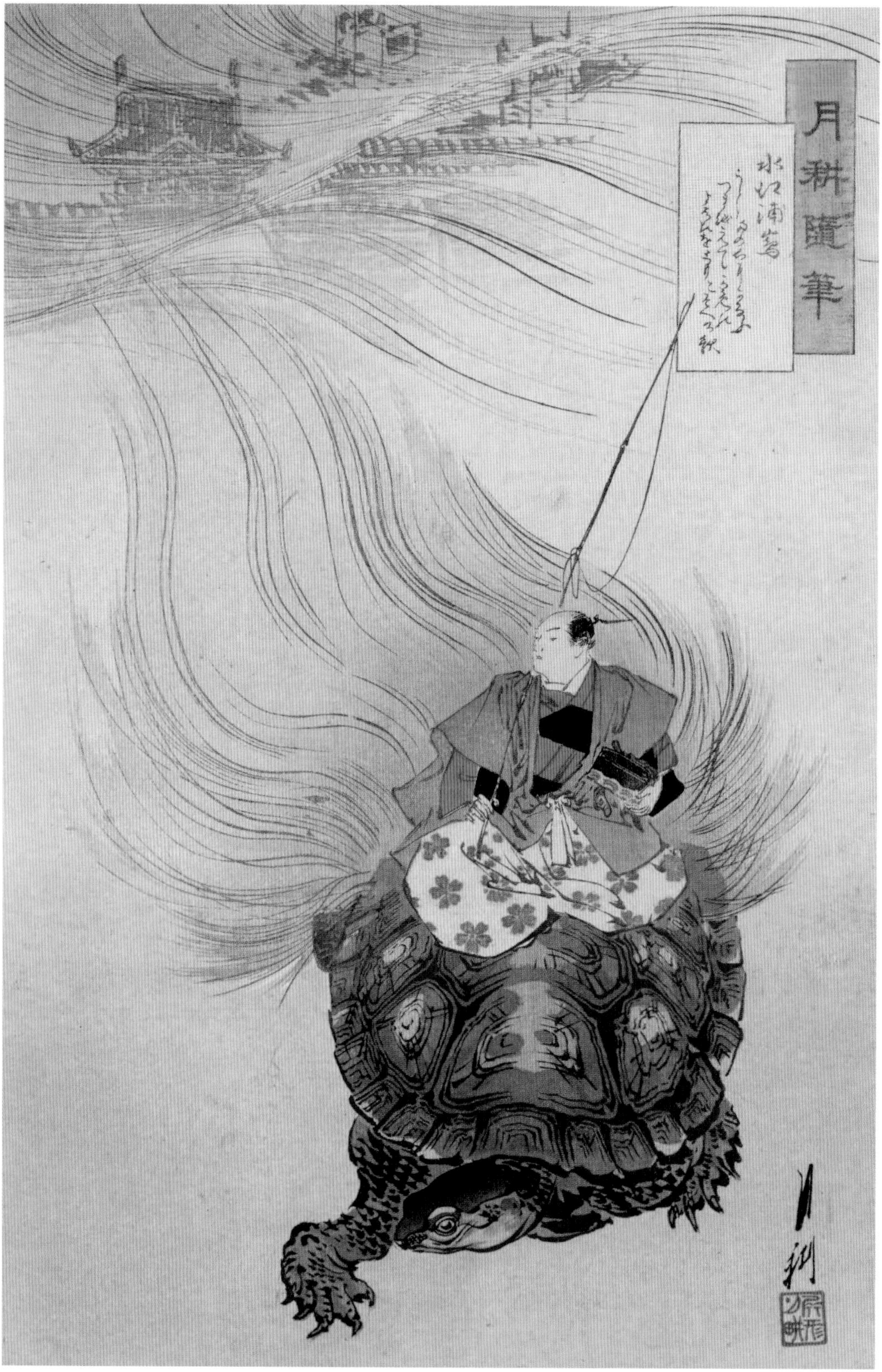
月耕隨筆
水江浦嶋

national textbooks. Along with the mythological history of the emperors discussed in previous chapters, the textbooks for younger students also incorporated native folk and fairy tales, many of which were selected from the *otogi-zōshi*.

The Tale of Urashima Tarō

The story of Urashima Tarō is from the core set of 'national fairy tales'. The story has undergone various changes from its origins as *Urashimako* in the *Nihon Shoki* and *Man'yōshū*, through the many different illustrated *otogi-zōshi* versions during the Muromachi period, to the children's story version of the Meiji period (1868–1912) and subsequent inclusion in textbooks. The story remains relevant today as it represents people who feel as though the world has left them behind, as well as providing inspiration for modern science fiction stories of time travel.

Once upon a time, a fisherman named Urashima Tarō came across a group of children tormenting a turtle on the beach. The kindly Urashima rescued the turtle and released it into the ocean. A few days later, when Urashima was out on his fishing boat, the turtle came back to him and told him that, as thanks for his help, it would carry him down to the undersea palace of Ryūjin, the water dragon deity. Urashima rode on the turtle's back down to Ryūgū-jō, the Dragon Palace, where he met the beautiful princess Otohime.

After a few days, Urashima grew homesick and wished to return to his family. As a parting gift, the princess gave him a jewelled *tamatebako* box and made him promise never to open it. However, when Urashima returned home, he was confused to find that everything was not as he remembered it. His house and his parents were nowhere to be seen, and he didn't recognize any of the people around him. 'Do you know of a man named Urashima Tarō?' he asked a passerby.' The person answered uncertainly, saying, 'The name rings a bell. They say a man by that name lived here centuries ago; he went out to sea one day and never returned.'

Shocked, Urashima forgot about Otohime's warning and opened the lid of the box. As soon as he did so, in a burst of smoke Urashima instantly aged into an extremely old man

OPPOSITE: **Urashima Tarō rides on the back of a sea creature.**

with white hair and a stooped frame. To his horror, Urashima discovered that in the three days he had been in the palace beneath the waves, 300 years had passed up on the land. He staggered, his ancient eyes looking out to sea, then fell dead upon the sands. Across the waves came the voice of Otohime whispering, 'It was your old age contained within the box.'

The Tale of Momotarō or The Little Peach Boy

Momotarō, or Peach Boy, is a popular folk hero beloved to Japanese children. However, this seemingly benign legend has been used for purposes beyond simple entertainment. Like Urashima Tarō, the story of Momotarō was incorporated into the Japanese national curriculum as one of the country's native legends that represented the kind of national spirit and identity the government wanted to cultivate among the populace. The figure of Momotarō fighting against demons was co-opted as early as the first Sino-Japanese War in 1894, with the *oni* representing the Chinese, and later in the Russo-Japanese War of 1904 with the demons being the Russians. By World War II, Momotarō's foes became the Allies and the United States, and there was a flurry of cartoons featuring him as a war propaganda icon. The story has been translated into English many times, starting with A. B. Mitford's version in

1871. Just as it went through various reinterpretations in its native Japanese, so has it been retranslated and rewritten in English, often under the name *Little Peachling* or *Peach Boy*.

Once upon a time, an old woman was washing her clothes in the stream when a huge peach floated by. Astonished by its size, the woman quickly scooped it up and hurried home with it to show to her husband. That night, the couple sat down together to enjoy a meal made from the ripe, delicious-looking fruit; but just as they were about to cut through the flesh, the peach split open and from it emerged a child who spoke to them with a smile: 'Don't be afraid! I have been sent by the gods to be your child, for they know how you have longed for one of your own.' The childless couple were overjoyed, and gave the boy the name Momotarō, with '*momo*' meaning 'peach'.

Momotarō grew big and strong, and when he reached adolescence, he told his parents that he wished to fight a group of demons who were terrorizing the local people. His mother gave him a supply of rice cakes, and he set out to find their island.

While on his journey, Momotarō was resting one day when a ferocious dog approached him. Growling and snarling, it demanded Momotarō hand over his rations. However, when the dog learned of Momotarō's mission, it agreed to join him – although not before getting half a rice cake out of the deal.

Not long after, the pair encountered a monkey. The monkey, too, asked to join the party on their mission, and Momotarō agreed. Later on, the trio met a pheasant. At first, the dog tried to attack it, but Momotarō intervened and the bird was welcomed into their merry band.

When they at last reached the coast, the group found a little boat, which they boarded and set sail in. Upon reaching the island they found the *oni*'s dark, fortified castle. Momotarō and his friends sneaked into the stronghold and entered into ferocious battle with the demons. Together, they destroyed many of the *oni*, while others fled in terror. When they reached the Demon King himself, he promptly surrendered and begged them to spare his life.

Momotarō freed the prisoners being kept in the castle and collected a tidy haul of treasure. Then the group set off home

OPPOSITE: A sculpture of Momotarō and his animal companions stands in front of Okayama Station in Okayama Prefecture.

ABOVE: **A print by artist Toyoharu Utagawa (1735–1814), who founded the Utagawa school of *ukiyo-e*, shows Momotarō and his friends conquering the demons.**

again, laden down with treasure and leading the Demon King along with them.

The whole land rejoiced and thanked Momotarō for ridding them of the demon scourge, and Momotarō's parents were able to live out their days in peace and comfort with the riches their son had brought them.

The Star Lovers

The story of Orihime and Hikoboshi is a tragic romance that stems from the Chinese myth of *The Cowherd and the Weaver Girl* and its associated Qixi Festival. It derives from the tendency of ancient peoples to worship natural celestial phenomena: Orihime is the star Vega and Hikoboshi is Altair, with the Celestial River being the Milky Way.

Tanabata, or the Star Festival, is one of the most prominent festivals in Japan, which takes place on 7 July at the height of summer. The colourful festival sees shopping districts decorated with vibrant streamers. People celebrate by writing their wishes on strips of coloured paper called *tanzaku* and tying these to bamboo plants or cuttings.

Orihime, whose name means 'Weaving Princess', was the daughter of Tentei the 'Sky King'. She would sit on the banks of the Celestial River weaving beautiful cloth for the gods. One day, she encountered Hikoboshi, the 'Cowherd Star', herding his oxen. It was love at first sight, and the two soon became inseparable. Like most young lovers, they were enamoured with one another to the exclusion of all else; Orihime stopped weaving her beautiful fabrics and Hikoboshi allowed his cows to roam free and uncontrolled across the plains of Heaven. Tentei was angered by this insolence and separated the couple on either side of the Amanogawa Celestial River, forbidding them to meet.

Heartbroken, Orihime begged her father to let her see her love and, swayed by his daughter's tears, Tentei agreed to allow the two to meet on the seventh day of the seventh month – providing that Orihime kept up with her weaving.

Orihime dedicated herself to her work and waited with excitement for their reunion. When the seventh day of the

BELOW: People write their wishes onto strips of colourful paper and hang them up during the Tanabata summer festival.

ABOVE: **This woodblock print by Shun'ei Katsukawa (1762–1819) makes striking use of red and black ink to depict Orihime and Hikoboshi standing on opposing sides of the Celestial River.**

seventh month arrived, a cloud of magpies gathered to form a fragile bridge across the Celestial River. There the two lovers spent a blissful day in one another's arms until they were forced to part again for another year.

Sadly, even an annual meeting is not a certainty; if it rains, the river becomes too wide for the magpie bridge to span, and the couple are forced to wait another whole year for the next opportunity. When it rains on Tanabata, the rains are called 'the tears of Orihime and Hikoboshi'.

Issun-bōshi

As with other such stories, the tale of Issun-bōshi, sometimes told in English as *The Inch-high Samurai*, evolved from its original form to the *otogi-zōshi* version and then changed again with Meiji-era rewritings as a children's fairy tale.

Some scholars think that the central idea for the pre-Muromachi era story originated with Sukunabikona, the Shinto deity of the *onsen* (hot springs), agriculture, healing, magic and sake; his name means 'small lord of renown'. He was the son of Kamimusubi, as well as the god who helped Ōkuninushi complete the construction of the land in an earlier chapter. There are also similarities with the popular English folklore character Tom Thumb, which is only one among many tales of tiny children told worldwide.

An old, childless couple went to pray at the shrine of the Empress Jingo that they might be blessed with a child. Happily, their wish was granted; but when the woman gave birth, they found that the child was only one *sun* (around 3cm/1in) tall and never grew any bigger. Thus, they named him Issun-bōshi, or 'one-*sun* boy'.

One day, Issun-bōshi decided that he wanted to become a warrior, and so he set out on his quest with a rice bowl for a boat, a chopstick for a paddle and a needle for a sword. He quickly found employment in the capital in a great mansion, where the occupants were delighted by his small stature, and he began to accompany the young lady of the household everywhere.

On a trip to a temple dedicated to the goddess Kannon, the young lady was set upon by a ferocious *oni*. Issun-bōshi immediately

BELOW: **Oni are traditionally depicted as ferocious creatures with red skin, sharp claws, horns, and wild eyes and hair.**

drew his needle-sword and challenged the demon, which merely laughed at him, opened its great mouth and swallowed the little man whole.

Issun-bōshi found himself in the dark cavern of the *oni*'s stomach, where he began to hack and slash with his tiny sword. The demon gave a cry of pain and coughed Issun-bōshi back up before fleeing to the mountains.

As they were about to set off back home, the young lady spied a mallet dropped by the fleeing *oni*. This happened to be a magical mallet that could grant wishes. Issun-bōshi promptly swung the mallet and uttered his wish, and suddenly he was six feet tall. Now a slightly-taller-than-average man and renowned hero, Issun-bōshi married the young lady and they lived a life of happiness and prosperity.

Kintarō the Golden Boy

The story of Kintarō, whose name means 'gold boy', is another that is familiar to all Japanese children. Mixing fact and fiction, it is supposedly based on Sakata Kintoki, a renowned samurai of Minamoto no Yorimitsu, the famous Heian period warrior who also makes a heroic appearance in the tale of Shuten-dōji. Children's Day is celebrated in Japan on 5 March, and it is customary for families to display a doll of Kintarō in the hope that their boys will grow to be as brave and strong as the folk hero. There is a shrine dedicated to him at the foot of Mount Ashigara in Hakone.

Kintarō grew up in the forests on Mount Ashigara. From a very young age, he showed incredible physical strength. He spent his days chopping down trees with his trusty axe and making friends with the animals of the forest, eventually learning to speak their language.

One day, when Kintarō and his animal friends were heading home, they came to a river they could not cross. With his bare hands, Kintarō pushed down a tree growing on the bank to form a bridge. Just as this happened, the famous warrior Minamoto no Yorimitsu was passing by and witnessed his feat of strength. Astounded by Kintarō's raw power, he took the boy under his wing and brought him back to live with him in Kyoto. There,

ISSUN-BŌSHI FOUND HIMSELF IN THE DARK CAVERN OF THE ONI'S STOMACH, WHERE HE BEGAN TO HACK AND SLASH WITH HIS TINY SWORD.

Kintarō changed his name to Sakata no Kintoki and studied martial arts, eventually rising to be one of Yorimitsu's chief samurai. He became known throughout the land as a great warrior, and tales of his heroic deeds awed and entertained children and adults alike.

The Three Great *Yōkai*

For there to be heroes, there must also be villains for them to defeat, and Japanese legends are filled with ferocious demons, ogres and other assorted *yōkai*. Among these, folklorist Kazuhiko Komatsu identified three as being the most feared of medieval Kyoto, and collectively named them the Three Great *Yōkai*.

Shuten-dōji

During the reign of Emperor Ichijō, people started going missing from the capital city of Kyoto, many of them young women. A divination was performed by a diviner of the imperial court, which determined that the culprit was a ferocious demon king, Shuten-dōji, who resided on Mount Ōe. The emperor commanded the warrior Minamoto no Yorimitsu (commonly known as Raikō) to take a band of warriors to eliminate the demon scourge.

The group departed and on their way to the mountain they encountered several old men who gave them useful information:

ABOVE: **The young Kintarō demonstrates his strength on Mount Ashigara, watched by Watanabe no Tsuna, one of Minamoto no Yorimitsu's samurai. Print by Kunisada Utagawa, 1811.**

ABOVE: Raikō, also known as Minamoto no Yorimitsu, beheads the terrifying yōkai Shuten-dōji. Print by Yoshitoshi Tsukioka (1839–1892).

the demon king was fond of alcohol and prone to drinking to excess. It later emerged that these men were deities in human form.

Raikō and his men disguised themselves as humble mountain ascetics, or *yamabushi*, and made their way to the demon's castle. There, they managed to convince the demon king to let them stay the night. For his part, Shuten-dōji seemed delighted to have an excuse to let the sake flow, and he was soon regaling the group with boastful tales as he gulped down alcohol like water.

Raikō took the opportunity to offer the demon king the sake he had received from the deities, which knocked Shuten-dōji out cold. Then, Raikō had his men hold the demon down while he cut off the creature's head – only for the severed head to continue to bite at him with its ferocious jaws. Raikō ultimately defended himself by wearing several of his men's helmets on top of his own until he could subdue the unruly head.

After that, a mighty battle ensued during which Raikō and his men slaughtered all the other demons in the castle. Once the horde was cleared, the triumphant warriors freed the imprisoned women and led them home to safety.

Tamamo-no-Mae

A stunningly beautiful and intelligent woman, who also happened to be a nine-tailed fox spirit, or *kitsune*, Tamamo-no-Mae was the favourite courtesan of Emperor Toba. Before she came to Japan, she is said to have wreaked havoc as far afield as

China and India, always disguising herself as a gorgeous woman to seduce powerful leaders and bring them down.

No sooner had she become the emperor's consort than he fell gravely ill with no apparent cause. An *onmyōji*, or diviner, was called in, who saw through Tamamo-no-Mae's disguise. She promptly disappeared from court, causing a great army to be sent in her pursuit. Eventually, they caught up to her in fox form and she was shot dead, taking one arrow to the flank and one through the throat.

A later addition to the story described how when the fox-woman was killed, her spirit transformed into a stone named the Sessho-seki, or Killing Stone, from which issued noxious gasses.

LEFT: **The warrior Miura-no-suke confronts Tamamo-no-mae as she transforms into a nine-tailed fox. Woodblock print by Gakutei Yashima (1786–1868).**

Later, a Buddhist priest performed an exorcism on the stone and Tamamo-no-Mae was pacified.

This rock is located in Tochigi Prefecture in the volcanic Nasu mountains, an area famed for its hot springs that often sees volcanic gases spouting forth from the ground. However, on 5 March 2022, local news reported that the Sessho-seki had spontaneously split apart. Internet rumours abounded that the spirit of Tamamo-no-Mae had been released to wreak havoc on the world once more, and at the end of the month, the local government had priests conduct a purification ceremony to once again appease the spirit.

The appeal of a seductive female villain is seen throughout cultures worldwide, and it is no surprise that Tamamo-no-Mae has enjoyed enduring popularity, from portrayals in Noh and kabuki plays to appearances as a fox-eared anime girl in the *Fate/Grand Order* mobile game.

Ōtakemaru

Ōtakemaru was not simply an *oni*, but a *kijin* – an *oni* so powerful that he was both demon and god. He lived in the Suzuka Mountains, a range that runs through central Japan, during the reign of Emperor Kanmu. During this time, he terrorized the locals and stole tributes bound for the emperor in Kyoto. Eventually, the emperor commanded his shogun, Sakanoue no Tamuramaro, to kill the demon. The shogun took his army into the mountains, but their search was hampered by a great storm summoned by Ōtakemaru.

In the same mountains there also lived a beautiful goddess by the name of Suzuka Gozen. When Ōtakemaru laid eyes on her, he became enchanted by her beauty and was desperate to spend a night with her. He transformed himself into various disguises, including a handsome young man and a court noble, but every attempt at winning over her affections was rebuffed.

In the meantime, Sakanoue prayed to the Buddhist gods to help him find the demon, and in his sleep, he received a vision that told him he must seek the help of Suzuka Gozen. The next day, he sent his men away and journeyed alone into the mountains until he came to a palace where he was welcomed by a beautiful woman,

OPPOSITE: **Sakanoue no Tamuramaro was a famous warrior during the early Heian period.**

ABOVE: **Huge *nebuta* floats depicting warriors, kabuki actors, gods, and mythical figures are carried through the streets during the Nebuta Matsuri in Aomori Prefecture.**

with whom he spent the night. She told him that she had been sent down from Heaven to help him slay the demon, and together they hatched a plan.

When Ōtakemaru next came to the palace, Suzuka Gozen asked for his powerful swords to defend herself from a warrior who had threatened her life, and he complied, giving her two of his three blades. Then, when he returned the next night, Sakanoue was waiting for him. Ōtakemaru transformed into his true form, a ferocious demon standing 10m (33ft) tall with shining eyes. A furious battle commenced between the two that shook both Heaven and Earth as each fought with everything he had. At last Sakanoue, backed by the holy protection of the thousand-armed Kannon and Bishamonten, the god of war, prevailed, lopping off the head of the *oni* in one fell swoop.

After he brought back the severed head of the demon, the emperor rewarded Sakanoue with titles and land, and he and Suzuka Gozen married and lived happily ever after.

The Nebuta Matsuri, held in Aomori Prefecture during the summer, is said to be inspired by this legend and Sakanoue no

Tamuramaro's other campaigns to exterminate *oni*, which in reality probably refer to his efforts to subdue local hostile tribes at the time. The *nebuta* are large, colourful paper floats of brave warriors and gods that are carried through the streets in riotous processions.

The Forty-seven *Rōnin*

The revenge of the Forty-seven *rōnin* is a historical event that subsequently gained legendary status. It is a defining piece of samurai history that exemplifies the *bushidō* warrior code by which samurai were supposed to live.

The Lead-up

The tale begins in 1701, when two *daimyo* (feudal lords) were tasked with receiving the envoy of Emperor Higashiyama at Edo Castle. Asano Takumi-no-Kami Naganori was lord of the Akō Domain, and Kamei Korechika was lord of the Tsuwano Domain. Both were taking their requisite year in the capital of Edo under the system of *sankin-kōtai*, whereby vassals of the shogun were required to spend alternate years in the city as a way to strengthen the shogunate's control of the country.

In preparation, the two regional *daimyō* were being instructed in etiquette by Kira Kozuke-no-Suke Yoshinaka, a high-ranking official in the Tokugawa Tsunayoshi's shogunate. Kira, whether disappointed with his charges or simply because he was malicious, insulted them mercilessly for what he saw as their failure to show proper deference to him. Instead of teaching, he spent his time ridiculing the two men for his own entertainment.

Asano, seeing it as his duty, bore this disrespect without complaint. Kamei, however, was incensed, and that night he declared to his councilors, 'Tomorrow, when I return to court, I will slay that wretched man!'

Naturally, Kamei's followers endorsed their lord, but one wise member of the bunch was troubled by the consequences of this plan. That night, he slipped out and took a large bribe over to Kira, presenting it as a token of gratitude from his lord for Kira's instruction.

A FURIOUS BATTLE COMMENCED BETWEEN THE TWO THAT SHOOK BOTH HEAVEN AND EARTH AS EACH FOUGHT WITH EVERYTHING HE HAD.

When Kamei arrived at court the next morning, still fuming and ready to kill the official, he found Kira's attitude transformed; he was suddenly polite and obsequious, taking every opportunity to humble himself before Kamei. Seeing this, Kamei's bloodthirst deserted him, and he and his house were spared what could have been their end.

Asano, however, had not sent any gifts to grease Kira's wheels, and so Kira treated him even worse than before. His insults escalated, until finally he said to Asano, 'You are nothing but a countryside boor, ignorant in the refined customs and manners of Edo.'

This was the final straw for Asano; he drew his dagger and attacked Kira, chasing him down the beautiful panelled corridor of the castle. However, his strikes missed their target and only grazed Kira's cheek. He was quickly overtaken by guards and arrested. Although he had not badly injured Kira, the punishment for an attack on an official within the bounds of Edo

BELOW: **Asano Naganori leads the forty-seven rōnin in their assault on Kira Yoshinaka.**

Castle was serious. Asano was ordered to commit *hara-kiri*, or self-disembowelment, his lands were taken from his family, and his retainers were made *rōnin* – wandering masterless samurai.

Among Asano's retainers, his principal counsellor, Ōishi Kuranosuke Yoshio, was a particularly loyal man. He and 46 others of Asano's men swore a secret oath to avenge their master, despite knowing that it would lead to their deaths. Thus began the scheming for a plot that would capture the imagination of Japan, and later the world, for generations.

The Revenge

After taking down Asano, Kira was wary of retaliation, so he surrounded himself with armed guards and sent spies to Kyoto, where Ōishi had settled, to keep an eye on him.

ABOVE: **Act eleven of the Chūshingura, when the rōnin pursue the guards at Kira's home.**

While some of the other men went undercover as craftsmen and merchants, Ōishi, to all intents and purposes, gave his life over to drunkenness and debauchery. He divorced his loyal wife and sent her away with his children. He frequented taverns and pleasure houses and let himself be seen behaving shamelessly. One night, a man from Satsuma came across Ōishi lying drunk in the street and, recognizing him, he laughed scornfully, calling him unworthy of the title 'samurai'. He kicked and spat at Ōishi, telling him that he was craven and without honour for failing to avenge his lord and instead giving himself over to women and wine.

Eventually, after more than a year with no sign of an attempt on his life, Kira gradually relaxed his guard. Now, the other *ronin* surreptitiously gathered in Edo, and in their roles as craftsmen, gained access to Kira's house and learned its layout and the temperaments of his men.

After two years, Ōishi slipped away from Kyoto and met the other *ronin* at a secret meeting place in Edo. On the dark, cold night of 31 January 1703, the men gathered one last time. They shared a meal and pledged themselves once more to their task. Ōishi gave an impassioned speech to his men, during which he called for them not to take any innocent lives in the upcoming conflict. 'Tonight, we attack our enemy and have our revenge! But there is no honour in killing the old and the vulnerable, so take heed not to kill a single helpless old man, woman or child.'

At the appointed time, the *ronin* simultaneously launched their attack in two groups, one storming the front of the estate and one the back. After a fierce fight at the front entrance, the two groups joined up inside and together fought Kira's samurai. Any who tried to escape to get help were shot down by archers Ōishi had posted on the roof. During all this, Kira had taken refuge in a closet on the veranda with his wife and female servants.

When the *ronin* fought their way to Kira's chambers, they found his three strongest and most loyal men at the door. There ensued a bitter fight where Kira's men were able to hold off the entire band of *ronin* until Ōishi rallied them, reminding them that they had vowed to lay down their lives to avenge their lord. Yet when all of Kira's men were slain and the *ronin* searched the house, they could find no sign of their quarry.

Kira's Death

Just as the *ronin* were starting to despair that their target had managed to escape, a secret exit was discovered behind a hanging scroll that led out to a courtyard containing a small storage shed. Upon inspection, two guards jumped out and were quickly slain before a third man was discovered, crouched and trembling in the back. The alert whistle was sounded, and when Ōishi arrived he confirmed that the man was Kira; the scar on his cheek was extra proof, as the remnant of Asano's attack.

OPPOSITE: **The rōnin discover Kira's hiding place.**

FOR THEIR CRIMES OF VIOLENT MURDER, THEY WERE SENTENCED TO PERFORM HARA-KIRI.

Ōishi got down on his knees and addressed Kira with the respect befitting a man of his station: 'My lord, we are the retainers of Asano Takumi-no-Kami. Last year your lordship and our master quarrelled in the palace, and our master was sentenced to *hara-kiri*, and his family was ruined. We have come tonight to avenge him, as is the duty of faithful and loyal men. I pray your lordship to acknowledge the justice of our purpose. And now, my lord, we beseech you to perform *hara-kiri*. I myself shall have the honour to act as your second, and when, with all humility, I shall have received your lordship's head, it is my intention to lay it as an offering upon the grave of Asano Takumi-no-Kami.'

Ōishi was offering Kira an honourable and noble death, but no matter how many times he entreated Kira, the other man simply cowered in silent fear. In the end, the *rōnin* held Kira down and Ōishi sliced off his head with the same dagger that Asano had used to perform *hara-kiri*. The *rōnin* were victorious.

Aftermath

As planned, the band of men now set out for Sengaku-ji Temple, blood-covered and triumphant. On the way, many people marvelled at the loyalty and courage of these men who had fought with such honour. At the temple, they took the severed head to their lord's tomb and laid it there as an offering.

Soon after, they were called to the supreme court, and the verdict was passed: for their crimes of violent murder, they were sentenced to perform *hara-kiri*. Nonetheless, the Forty-seven had been resolved to this fate from the outset, and they went nobly to their deaths.

The *rōnin* were buried in front of their lord's tomb, and as word of their story spread, people flocked to pray before the graves of the faithful men. Among them was a man who flung himself before Oishi's grave and begged his forgiveness, saying, 'When I saw you lying drunk by the roadside in Kyoto, I knew nothing of your true plan to avenge your lord. Thinking you a man without a sliver of honour, I kicked you and spat upon you. I am here now to ask for your pardon and to offer my atonement.' With that, the man stabbed himself in the stomach and died, after which he was buried beside the 47 *rōnin*.

Their graves are still standing at Sengaku-ji Temple in the
Shinagawa district of Tokyo, along with a museum dedicated
to the incident. A festival is held annually on 14 December to
commemorate the Forty-seven *rōnin* and their enduring legacy.

ABOVE: **The tombs of
the forty-seven rōnin
can still be seen at
Sengaku-ji Temple in
the Shinagawa district of
Tokyo.**

Chūshingura

Fictionalized retellings of the incident of the Forty-seven *rōnin*
have become such a huge and popular genre that it has its own
name: *Chūshingura*. The title, literally meaning 'The Treasury of
Loyal Retainers', is given to accounts in literature, theatre, film
and other media.

Kanadehon Chūshingura, a *bunraku* puppet play, was first
performed in 1748 with a kabuki version produced later. The
story made its film debut in 1907, with many other versions soon
after. With its themes of dedication and loyalty, the story captured

the imagination of the people, which also served the modern Japanese government's efforts to craft a *kokutai*, or national identity, that was centred around worship of and fidelity to the divine emperor. In 1941, Kenji Mizoguchi was commissioned by the Japanese military to make a film version that would boost morale and support for the war. Performances of the story were briefly banned during the USA's occupation of Japan after World War II because of its glorification of militarism and feudalistic concepts of honour and loyalty.

The story is also well-known in the West through translations and popular culture. Despite the Hollywood film *47 Ronin* starring Keanu Reeves in 2012 taking many liberties with the original story and being a box office bomb, it has nevertheless played a part in the story's evolution and in keeping it alive around the world.

BELOW: **The 1962 film *Chūshingura: Hana no Maki, Yuki no Maki* is one of many adaptations of the tale of the forty-seven rōnin across various media.**

The tale of the 47 *rōnin* is a prime example of how a real event can become mythologized through storytelling, elevating the participants to legendary status, and subsequently be reworked and used for political purposes, just like those original myths in the *Kojiki*.

Seppuku and Shinjū

The ritual suicide the *rōnin* undertook is called *seppuku*, with the physical act referred to as *hara-kiri* (literally 'stomach-cutting'). It was a way for samurai to die with honour, according to their *bushidō* code, and would later also be practised by military servicemen and nationalists. After performing *seppuku*, the warrior would be decapitated by an assistant. The earliest recorded example is by Minamoto no Yorimasa, a poet, warrior and Buddhist priest, at the beginning of the Genpei War in 1180. Legend has it that Yorimasa's retainer took his severed head, fastened it to a rock and threw it into the Uji River so that it could not be found by his enemies.

ABOVE: **Keanu Reeves starred in *47 Ronin*, a 2013 Hollywood retelling of the famous story.**

Like a fossil tree
From which we gather no flowers
Sad has been my life
Fated no fruit to produce
– Yorimasa's death poem

Another form of ritual suicide that features in Japanese stories is *shinjū*, or double suicide. In 1703 this captured the imagination of the public when the famous *bunraku* puppet play *The Love Suicides at Sonezaki* by Chikamatsu Monzaemon was written within a few weeks of the real incident it was based on.

It tells the sad tale of Tokubei, a young merchant, and Ohatsu, a prostitute. Tokubei is in love with Ohatsu and hopes to buy her

芳年武者无類

源三位頼政

freedom; however, his family have secretly planned for him to marry another woman and already accepted her family's dowry. When Tokubei rejects the marriage, he is disowned and told to pay back the money. Unfortunately, he has lent it to a merchant named Kuheiji, a villainous man who refuses to pay the amount back and implies that he will use it to redeem Ohatsu's contract himself. Tokubei feels that he has shamed his family beyond redemption and, seeing no other way out of their situation, the couple choose to die together.

Lovers believed that they would be reunited in Heaven, which was supported by the teachings of Pure Land Buddhism and other feudal beliefs in the Edo period (1603–1868). The play solidified this idea in the public's mind and was so influential that it inspired a spate of double suicides following its debut.

Kamikaze

The spirit of samurai honour and willingness to die in service to one's leader would be revived with the Meiji government's re-establishment of imperial rule and its push to construct a cohesive national identity (*kokutai*) through the promotion of Shinto and other 'traditional' Japanese beliefs and values. During the pre-war and war years, old tales of bravery and heroism, such as the

OPPOSITE: **Woodblock print of Minamoto no Yorimasa, part of Tsukioka Yoshitoshi's Courageous Warriors series, published from 1883–6.**

LEFT: **Kamikaze pilots prepare for battle during World War II.**

ABOVE: **Author and right-wing nationalist Yukio Mishima took inspiration from the kamikaze pilots and the samurai that came before them.**

47 *rōnin* and Momotarō, were widely popularized, and Japan's creation myths were also re-embedded in the public consciousness as a way to reinforce the validity of the emperor's divine lineage.

The origins of the term 'kamikaze' have already been discussed in the chapter on deities, but centuries later the word also came to be used for a modern form of 'divine wind': the name was given to a special attack unit who piloted suicide missions towards the end of the Pacific War. Kamikaze pilots were hailed as heroes and enshrined at Yasukuni Shrine, where the emperor paid homage to them twice a year. Stories of the heroism and bravery of kamikaze pilots were disseminated to encourage volunteers to sign up, of which there was no shortage.

In the post-war years, there has still been a tendency to mythologize the suicide pilots, although there have also been outspoken critics. In 2006, the then-editor-in-chief of the Yomiuri Shimbun newspaper was quoted as saying: 'It's all a lie that they left filled with braveness and joy, crying, "Long live the emperor!" They were sheep at a slaughterhouse.' Controversy still surrounds Yasukuni Shrine as over a thousand convicted war criminals are enshrined there along with almost 2.5 million others who have died in service to Japan.

Yukio Mishima, the celebrated author and right-wing nationalist, was inspired by the tales of the samurai and kamikaze to stage an unsuccessful coup in 1970, which ended with his cry of 'Long live the emperor!' as he performed *seppuku*.

This serves as a powerful reminder of how myth and legend can be manipulated by those who seek to use them to disseminate particular ideologies, and of how deep-rooted and insidious such beliefs can become.

Poetry

As well as fiction, Japan also has a long and enduring tradition of poetry; poems, or the act of composing poetry, feature prominently in many mythical tales reaching back to the *Kojiki* and *Nihon Shoki*. Poetry was a courtly pursuit, but it was also composed by those outside the court including monks, farmers and warriors.

Waka

While the haiku is most commonly known overseas, *waka* is the main traditional form that can be seen in the *Kojiki*. Classical *waka* poetry consists of a number of different forms that have evolved and developed over the centuries.

The Man'yōshū

The oldest collection of Japanese *waka* poetry is the *Man'yōshū*, or the *Collection of Ten Thousand Leaves*, compiled in the 8th century during the Nara period (710–94). It contains more than 4,500 poems by a huge variety of authors from different walks of life. The topics cover Shinto, Buddhist, Confucian and Daoist themes, as well as nature, romance and reflections on death and loss.

It also features more than 150 species of grasses and trees, which have inspired the *Man'yō* garden, a themed botanical garden that includes every mentioned species, rather like a Shakespeare garden.

> *At the beginning of heaven and earth*
> *The eight hundred, the thousand myriads of gods,*
> *Assembled in high council On the shining beach of the*
>   *Heavenly River,*
> *Consigned the government of the Heavens*
> *Unto the Goddess Hirume, the Heaven-Illumining One,*
> *And the government for all time,*

As long as heaven and earth endured,
Of the Rice-abounding Land of Reed Plains
Unto her divine offspring,
Who, parting the eightfold clouds of the sky,
Made his godly descent upon the earth.

As the moon sinks on the mountain-edge
The fishermen's lights flicker
Far out on the dark wide sea.
When we think that we alone
Are steering our ships at midnight.
We hear the splash of oars
Far beyond us.

Ono no Komachi

A *waka* poet in the early Heian period, Ono no Komachi was renowned not only for her literary talent, but also her incredible beauty. She is one of the *Rokkasen*, or Six Poetry Immortals, as well as the *Sanjūrokkasen*, or 36 Immortals of Poetry, that later supplanted that list.

BELOW: Pages from Volume 9 of the Man'yōshū, held at Kyoto National Museum.

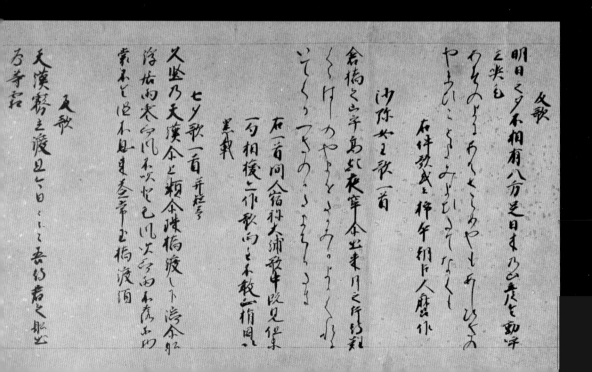

Some of the poetry exchanged between Komachi and her myriad lovers can be found in the *Kokin Wakashū*, or *Collection of Japanese Poems of Ancient and Modern Times*, an imperial anthology of *waka* poetry dating from around 905.

While there are poems that are clearly attributed to her, the actual historical figure of Komachi is a mysterious one, with nothing about her life being known for certain. There are many legends surrounding her, some of which have provided inspiration for later Noh plays. Many of these surround her romantic escapades, some depict her sensuality while others describe her cruelty. Others follow an older Komachi whose beauty has faded and who now regrets her previous fickle nature. Yukio Mishima's modern reworking of her legend, *Sotoba Komachi*, brings the character into the modern era, placing her in the salons and ballrooms of Meiji Japan.

Komachi's poems are generally melancholy in tone and lament the fleetingness of life and of beauty.

> *A life in vain.*
> *My looks, talents faded*
> *like these cherry blossoms*
> *paling in the endless rains*
> *that I gaze out upon, alone.*

Renga

Meaning 'linked verse', *renga* is a form of collaborative poetry that became particularly popular at court during the Muromachi period. It has its origins in the *Kojiki* and the story of the semi-legendary Prince Yamato Takeru.

As a young man, Prince Yamato Takeru slew his older brother, Prince Ōusu, for failing to heed their father's imperial summons. Fearful of his son's temper, the Emperor Keikō sent Prince Takeru to subdue enemies of the court in the south and the west.

First, Prince Takeru went to the land of Kumaso in the west. There, he dressed in women's clothing and presented as such a beautiful woman that the local clan leader took him as his future wife. After the wedding feast, when the newly-wed couple were left alone to consummate the marriage, Prince Takeru threw off

THE ACTUAL HISTORICAL FIGURE OF KOMACHI IS A MYSTERIOUS ONE, WITH NOTHING ABOUT HER LIFE BEING KNOWN FOR CERTAIN.

his feminine garb, revealing his true identity and a hidden sword, and killed the chieftain on the bridal bed. He then sang a victory poem and the region submitted to the emperor's authority.

In the south, Prince Takeru was surprised to find a warm welcome waiting for him. Still, he was dedicated to his mission, and the next day he invited the chieftain to spar, having secretly replaced the man's sword with a wooden blade. During their match, the chieftain's sword broke and Prince Takeru slayed him.

Next, Emperor Keikō sent his son to the east. Before setting out, Prince Takeru went to visit his aunt, Yamatohime, the high priestess of Amaterasu at Ise Grand Shrine. She gave him the sword Kusanagi, the very same that had been found by Susano-wo in the body of the eight-headed serpent, and that eventually became one of the Three Imperial Regalia.

On his journey eastwards, Prince Takeru and his men were beset by a terrible storm as they sailed across the body of water now known as Tokyo Bay. Prince Takeru's wife, Oto-Tachibanahime, said that the storm had been sent by the sea god Watatsumi, and she gave herself to the waters as a sacrifice. The storm immediately cleared and the prince was able to sail safely to land.

In the east, Prince Takeru successfully killed many enemies, but he still grieved for his lost wife. As he passed Mount Tsukuba, he met an old man and together they composed a poem.

Prince Takeru recited:
How many nights have I slept
Since passing Nihibari and Tsukuba?

And the old man answered:
Oh! The full count, I think
Is of nights nine
and of days ten

OPPOSITE: Ono no Komachi regards her own reflection in a woodblock print by Shuntei Katsukawa (1770–1820).

On the way home, Prince Takeru went hunting on Mount Ibuki and shot a boar which, unbeknown to him, turned out to be the *kami* of the mountain. Angered at being shot, the *kami* cursed the prince and Takeru fell gravely ill. Whenever his men

tried to encourage him, he would recite a poem, each one sadder than the last. Upon composing the fourth poem, the prince died.

After his death, Prince Takeru's spirit turned into a white bird that flew away, stopping at several locations before disappearing heavenward. Shrines were built in these places and are known as the Shiratori (White Bird) Shrines.

Haiku

Haiku, a short poetry form consisting of 17 syllables arranged in a 5-7-5 pattern, is closely associated with Buddhism. The most famous haiku poet of all time is the Buddhist monk Matsuo Bashō. Many of his poems are observational; they capture a scene in a few clean, evocative words, and reflect the principles of Zen Buddhism. A century after his death, Bashō was deified by the imperial government and the Shinto bureaucracy, and he is still revered as a saint of poetry today. His poems can be found carved into monuments all over Japan.

'Old pond
A frog jumps in –
The sound of water'

OPPOSITE: **Statue of prince Yamato Takeru in the gardens at Kanazawa Castle in Ishikawa Prefecture.**

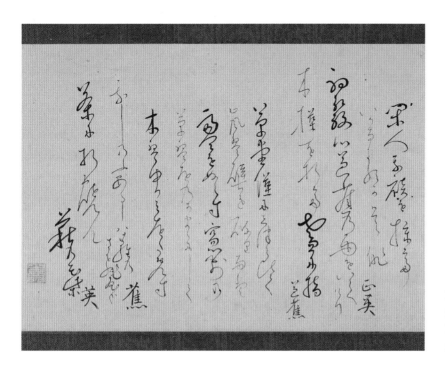

LEFT: **A haiku exchange penned by Matsuo Bashō, Japan's most famous haiku poet.**

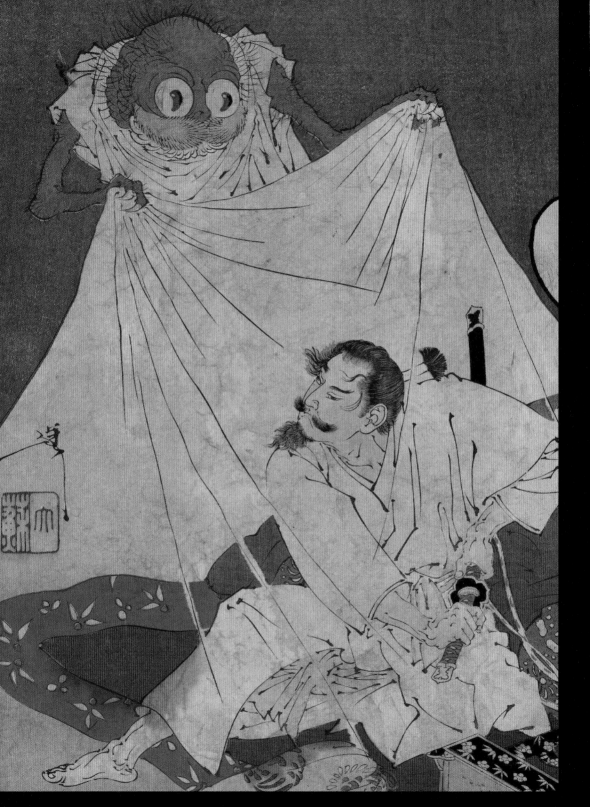

4

MYTHOLOGICAL CREATURES AND OBJECTS

There is no shortage of mythical creatures in Japanese folklore and legend. The general term given to this wide variety of supernatural beings is *yōkai*, which encompasses a range of creatures from the mundane-turned-mystical to the outright outlandish. *Yōkai* often have animal features, but may also appear human-like, while others are pure spirits with no discernible shape.

Setsuwa

The term *setsuwa* means 'spoken story', which is a form of oral storytelling that includes myths, legends, folk tales and anecdotes. As well as more general secular and native *setsuwa*, a large proportion of these tales are Buddhist *setsuwa* that include themes of karma and other Buddhist teachings. After being passed down orally, many *setsuwa* were later recorded in written forms, many of which were compiled by Buddhist monks during the Heian (794–1192) and Kamakura (1192–1333) periods. The oldest known collection is the *Nihon Ryōiki*, or the *Record of Miraculous Events in*

OPPOSITE: **A print by Yoshitoshi Tsukioka (1839–1892) features a** *tsuchigumo,* **a spider-like yokai.**

Japan, which was written in the 8th or 9th century and contains 116 Buddhist-themed tales.

Konjaku Monogatarishū

The collection *Konjaku Monogatarishū*, or *Anthology of Tales from the Past*, comprises over 1,000 stories written during the late Heian period. The tales are set in India, China and Japan, reflecting the path that Buddhism took within these countries, and the content is drawn from Buddhist texts and popular folklore. There are few mythological or Shinto themes; instead, the focus is on the spread of Buddhism, its dogma and teachings, and on encounters between humans and supernatural forces.

Through popular dissemination and countless retellings, many of the stories have taken a firm hold in the general public consciousness. The Akira Kurosawa film *Rashomon* (1950) is based on the short story *In a Grove* by Akutagawa Ryūnosuke.

E-hon and Emakimono

'*E*' means 'picture', and there are various forms of picture-based and highly illustrated narratives within Japanese art and

BELOW: Pages from the *Konjaku Monogatarishū*, a collection of tales compiled during the late Heian period.

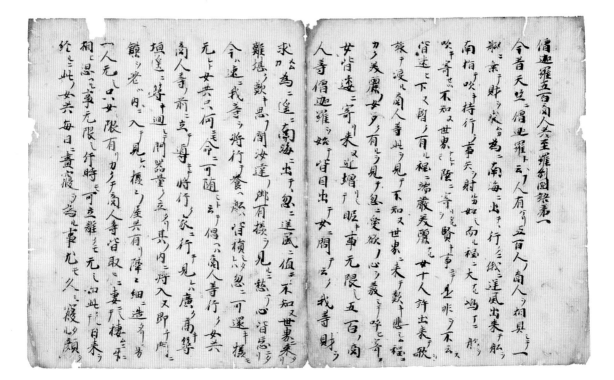

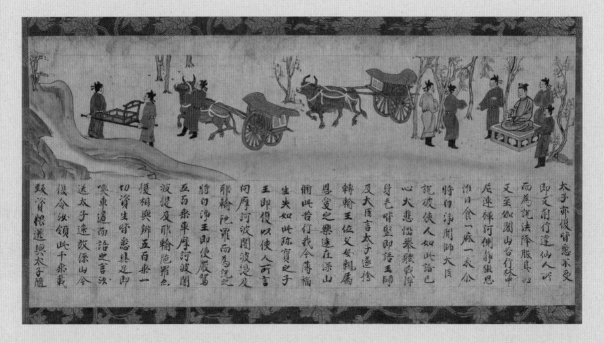

literature. *Emakimono* are illustrated horizontal narrative scrolls that combine calligraphy and illustration to tell epic tales. Often commissioned by aristocrats or Buddhist temples, the art form particularly flourished during the Kamakura era until *otogi-zōshi* became the more popular form of illustrated storytelling in the Muromachi period (1338–1477).

E-hon simply means 'picture book', but it also refers specifically to a type of woodblock printed, illustrated book published during the Edo period (1603–1868). This form developed from the earlier *Nara-ehon*, which often consisted of *otogi-zōshi* stories.

Ukiyo-e

Ukiyo-e is probably the best-known genre of Japanese art internationally. The term translates to 'pictures of the floating world' and refers to a style of woodblock prints and paintings produced during the Edo period. This developed around the *ukiyo* urban lifestyle and culture in the capital of Edo (present-day Tokyo) and dealt with subjects such as beautiful women, landscapes, kabuki actors, scenes from history and folk tales, and erotica. Under the broader umbrella of *ukiyo-e*, the subgenre *yūrei-zu* encompasses images of ghosts and other supernatural beings. The series *One Hundred Ghost Stories* by Katsushika Hokusai

ABOVE: The *Illustrated Sutra of Past and Present Karma* is a Buddhist scripture that tells of the lives of the Buddha.

brings the *yōkai* and superstitions of Edo-period Japan to life in bold, colourful prints that depict scenes from popular ghost stories of the time.

Gazu Hyakki Yagyō

Published in 1776 and followed by three sequel works, the *Gazu Hyakki Yagyō* is an *e-hon* by artist Toriyama Sekien that deals with the supernatural. The term *hyakki yagyō* is an idiomatic expression that literally translates to 'night parade of a hundred demons' and is similar to the English word 'pandemonium'. The book is a bestiary of ghosts, spirits and monsters from Japanese folklore. It references the earlier *Hyakkai Zukan* picture scroll completed in 1737 by Sawaki Suushi. Both works had a profound impact on *yōkai* imagery and on the popularity of certain creatures among the general populace.

Tengu

Tengu are a type of mischievous mountain sprite that might be roughly translated as 'goblin' in English. They can be either benevolent or malicious: when given the proper respect, they may bestow the chosen person with supernatural powers, magical objects or knowledge of the mountains.

The characteristics and meaning associated with *tengu* have evolved over the centuries. Originally, *tengu* were traditionally depicted as having the characteristics of birds, such as feathers, wings or beaks; these are called *koten*. The form of *tengu* most commonly known today, however, is that of a humanoid creature with a bright red face, long bulbous nose, wild white hair and bulging eyes, known as *daitengu*.

Some of the earliest tales about *tengu* appear in the *Konjaku Monogatarishū*, where

OPPOSITE: **In addition to his famous landscapes, Katsushika Hokusai also made woodblock prints of yōkai.**

BELOW: **A traditional *tengu* mask with a red face, long nose, and bushy eyebrows.**

MINZOKUGAKU

Along with the writers and artists who have disseminated tales of mythological creatures and popularized *yōkai* across the centuries, scholars have also been important in the spread of *yōkai*. They have cultivated understanding of *yōkai*'s place within Japanese mythology, culture, art and society.

The late 19th century saw the establishment of Japanese native folkloristics, or *minzokugaku*, as an academic field in Japan. Much of the current academic insight into *yōkai*, particularly their prevalence in oral tradition from certain regions, can be credited to the efforts of these folklorists.

Folklorist Kunio Yanagita is photographed here on February 9, 1962 in Tokyo.

Kunio Yanagita (1875–1962)
Considered the father of modern Japanese folklore studies, Yanagita was instrumental in the founding of *minzokugaku*, and acted as a mentor to many other scholars. His genre-defining work focused on local traditions and the importance of the folklore and oral legends of ordinary people.

Kizen Sasaki (1886–1933)
A frequent collaborator with Yanagita, he is best-known for his writings on the oral traditions and folklore of Iwate Prefecture.

Shinobu Orikuchi (1887–1953)
Founder of the Japan Folklorists Society, he was active in various fields and his studies combined Japanese folklore, classical literature and Shinto.

Zenchū Nakahara (1890–1964)
Born on the island of Kumejima, Nakahara wrote extensively on Okinawan history and religion as well as the *Omoro sōshi*, a written collection of songs and poems that records an oral history of Okinawa and the Ryūkyū Kingdom.

Keigo Seki (1899–1990)
Working under Yanagita, Seki investigated the roots of Japanese folklore as well as their universal elements and developed a system to categorize folktales.

Tadashi Kanehisa (1906–1997)
A folklorist and linguist, Kanehisa researched the language and legends of the Amami Islands, part of the Ryukyus.

they are depicted as unpleasant troublemakers, tempting and forcing people away from the pious Buddhist path. In the Kamakura period, *tengu* became closely associated with the *yamabushi*, mountain ascetics who followed the practices of Shugendō. *Tengu* would be blamed for mysterious occurrences in the mountains, such as whispered voices or sudden landslides, and could confuse those trying to make their way through dangerous mountain passes.

By the Edo period, they were regarded more as spirits that could be placated with the right rituals. *Tengu* might even be worshipped as beneficial *kami* and the deities of sacred mountains. The Shimokitazawa Tengu Matsuri, or Goblin Festival, celebrates Setsubun with a procession that includes a float featuring a huge *tengu* mask and people dressed up as a fearsome crow-like *tengu* and a red-nosed *tengu*.

Tengu remain a popular subject of Japanese fiction and culture, and there is even a Unicode Emoji character featuring the traditional long-nosed red *tengu* face, named 'Japanese Goblin'.

The *Tengu's* magic cape

As well as tales of frightening, evil *tengu* trying to lure people from the path of goodness, there are many other humorous folk tales that depict humans getting the better of *tengu* through trickery.

Once upon a time, there lived a mischievous young man named Hikoichi. Hikoichi had heard rumours about a magical cape owned by a *tengu* – a long-nosed goblin – that dwelled in the mountains near his village. This was a 'cape of hiding' that made the wearer invisible. Hikoichi desperately wanted it, so he thought up a plan to steal it.

One day, Hikoichi went up the mountain. Peering into a plain bamboo rod, he shouted at the top of his voice, 'Aah, how amazing! I can see all the faraway towns. What a great sight!'

The *tengu* soon appeared and, staring curiously at the piece of bamboo, asked, 'Hey, Hikoichi. What's so great about that? Let me look at it.'

Hikoichi replied, 'Goodness, no. When you look through this, you can see far-off sights up close. There's nothing else in the world like it.'

THE... GOBLIN FESTIVAL, CELEBRATES SETSUBUN WITH A PROCESSION THAT INCLUDES A FLOAT FEATURING A HUGE *TENGU* MASK AND PEOPLE DRESSED UP AS A FEARSOME CROW-LIKE *TENGU* AND A RED-NOSED *TENGU*.

This made the *tengu* even more curious, so he pleaded, 'Oh please, Hikoichi. I'll let you use this cape of hiding in return.'

At this, delighted but not showing it, Hikoichi said, 'That's such a dirty cape; can it really make me disappear? Oh well, if you insist.' So he handed the bamboo rod to the *tengu* and received the hiding cape in return.

The *tengu* looked eagerly through one end of the bamboo, but saw nothing. 'I can't see a thing. How do you get it to work?' Then he realized he had been deceived and exclaimed, 'You've tricked me, haven't you?' But by this time, Hikoichi had disappeared down the mountain wearing the magic cape.

BELOW: **A statue of a** *tengu* **at Mount Takao, an important place for followers of Shugendō.**

Kamikakushi

Tengu are frequently blamed for a phenomenon known as *kamikakushi*, literally 'hiding away by the gods' but more often translated as 'spiriting away'. For centuries there have been tales of children and young people who suddenly disappear without a trace, only to turn up later dazed and disorientated but otherwise unharmed, telling tales of long-nosed men and other strange beings and worlds. Hirata Atsutane, a revered scholar of the Edo period who studied Japan's native Shinto as well as folk tales and literature, interviewed a victim of this phenomenon for his work *Senkyō ibun* (*Strange Tales from the Land of the Immortals*). The idea saw a resurgence with the huge success of the 2001 Studio Ghibli film *Spirited Away* (*Sen to Chihiro no Kamikakushi* in Japanese) and is a well-worn trope in fantasy and horror media.

Sōjōbō

The king of all *tengu* is Sōjōbō, one of the few named *tengu* with a distinctive personality. This huge and powerful *daitengu* lives on Mount Kurama and takes the physical appearance of a *yamabushi* mountain hermit with long white hair and a long nose. He is most famed for having supposedly taught the warrior Minamoto no Yoshitsune in martial arts at Kurama Temple when Yoshitsune was a boy. According to the *Heiji Monogatari*, written in the Kamakura era, it was Sōjōbō's instruction that enabled Yoshitsune to run and jump beyond the limits of human power. The 15th-century Noh play *Kurama-tengu* popularly dramatized the story.

Sarutahiko Ōkami

The *kami* Sarutahiko is considered to be the original inspiration for the popular appearance of the *daitengu*. He is the leader of the earthly *kunitsukami*, the patron of martial arts and god of crossroads, and a symbol of Misogi, the Shinto practice of ritual purification. He acted as a guide to Ninigi when the heavenly grandson descended to rule over the land. He is depicted as a giant man with a big beard, glowing eyes, a ruddy face and a long nose, who carries a jewelled spear.

Oni

Roughly translated to 'demon' or 'ogre' in English, although different from the purely evil demons of Western tradition, *oni* are fierce, villainous *yōkai* with supernatural powers who frequently appear as the antagonist in legendary heroic tales.

WALT DISNEY STUDIOS PRESENTS
A STUDIO GHIBLI FILM
MIYAZAKI'S
SPIRITED AWAY

ABOVE: **Hayao Miyazaki's** *Spirited Away* **was released in 2001 and has been an enduring international success.**

ABOVE: **An *oni* counts money in this print dating from 1900.**

Generic or named *oni* feature as villains in tales such as *Momotarō* and *Issun-bōshi*.

Thought to be Buddhist in origin, the *oni* administer hellish justice for King Enma. In the human world, they have destructive powers and can bring about disasters. They have a taste for human flesh and can swallow a person whole. They are often depicted with red or blue skin, wearing tiger-skin loin cloths, with one or two horns growing out of their heads. A person may be transformed into or reborn as an *oni* if they are exceptionally wicked.

The Setsubun festival involves throwing beans out of the door with a shout of '*Oni wa soto! Fuku wa uchi!*', which means 'Demons out! Luck, come in!' In architecture, *onigawara* roof tiles carved with the ferocious visages of *oni* are similar to gargoyles, and adorn roofs to ward away bad luck. *Oni* have been popular subjects of literature and art for centuries, and this fascination persists to the present day.

The Red Oni Who Cried

A modern children's fairy tale written by Hirosuke Hamada in 1933 paints a much sweeter picture of the supposedly fearsome *oni*. The story teaches children to be grateful for their true friends who value them for who they are.

Once upon a time, a kind-hearted demon known as Red Oni lived in the mountains. He desperately wanted to be friends with the humans he saw in the nearby village, but whenever they caught sight of him, they would run away, screaming in fright.

One day, Red Oni was talking to his friend Blue Oni and told him of his sadness. Blue Oni came up with a plan: 'I'll go down into the village and start causing mischief and mayhem. Then you come along and chase me away. The villagers will see that you're a good demon, and the children will want to play with you.'

Although Red Oni was nervous, they carried out the plan and it went exactly as Blue Oni had said it would. The villagers thanked Red Oni for saving them, and from then on, he was welcome in the village.

After a few days, Red Oni realized that he hadn't seen Blue Oni in a while, so he went over to his house. On the door he found a note that said, 'Dear Red Oni, If people find out that you are friends with the bad Blue Oni, they will become scared of you again, so I am leaving. I hope you will have a happy life with the children in the village. Goodbye. Your friend, Blue Oni.'

When Red Oni read the note, he cried and cried and cried; but his tears would not bring back his dear friend.

BELOW: **A** *netsuke* **figurine of a kappa from the mid-nineteenth century.**

Kappa

A kind of water sprite with a distinctive appearance, *kappa* have a greenish, humanoid body with webbed hands and feet and a turtle-like shell on their back. On the top of their

IT IS SAID THAT
KAPPA OFTEN
KIDNAP HUMANS
FOR A SPECIFIC
REASON – TO
STEAL THEIR
SHIRIKODAMA, A
MYTHICAL BALL
LOCATED INSIDE
THE ANUS THAT
MAY CONTAIN
THE SOUL.

head is a depression filled with water, surrounded by a ring of hair rather like a monk's tonsure. (Through some linguistic evolution, a modern bob cut hairstyle sans the bald crown is called *okappa* in Japanese.)

Kappa reside in ponds and rivers and are often blamed for people drowning in bodies of water. As such, they have been used to warn children of the dangers of water through scary stories in which *kappa* lure people to their deaths. They also take animals, in particular horses.

Kappa can also be amicable and slightly mischievous. If a person befriends a *kappa*, the creature may help perform tasks, for example, irrigating a farmer's rice field or teaching a person about their expertise in medicine and bone-setting.

One of the funniest aspects of an already rather hilarious-looking creature is an association with bottoms. It is said that *kappa* often kidnap humans for a specific reason – to steal their *shirikodama*, a mythical ball located inside the anus that may contain the soul.

Kappa possess great strength and skill in wrestling, but there is an easy way to defeat them. *Kappa* are polite to a fault; if you bow to one, it will be obliged to perform a deep bow in return. This will spill the water stored on its head, and the *kappa* will be stuck in place until the depression is refilled with water from its river or pond. Alternatively, it can be challenged to a sumo wrestling match. Cucumber is said to be the *kappa's* favourite food, and sushi rolls filled with cucumber are known as *kappamaki*.

Tōno in Iwate Prefecture is said to be particularly rife with *kappa*, especially the Kappabuchi Pool. Influential scholar and folklorist Kunio Yanagita visited the area and in 1910 he compiled the local oral traditions into a book called *Tōno Monogatari*, which solidified the area's reputation as a hotbed of the amphibious *yōkai*.

Sōgen Temple in Tokyo is more commonly known as Kappa-dera, thanks to its location in Kappabashi. As a mascot of the area, *kappa* statues can be found throughout the grounds, and offerings of cucumbers are left at the shrine. The temple houses what is said to be the mummified arm of a *kappa*. Along with some other *yōkai*, the *kappa* (or parts of it) was a popular subject

of sideshows during the 19th century and earlier; there is even
indication that the idea for P. T. Barnum's Fiji mermaid may have
come from similar creations produced in China and Japan.

ABOVE: **Kappabuchi
Pool in Tono, Iwate
Prefecture, is said to be
home to many *kappa*.**

The Kappa's Promise

Long ago, a *kappa* dwelt in the waters of the River Kawachi.
He was a nuisance who seized the local livestock and even the
occasional villager. One day, a horse ventured near the river. The
kappa leapt upon it, but the horse struggled, twisting the *kappa*'s
neck and causing it great pain. But the *kappa* was stubborn, and
he clung on to the horse even as it dragged itself out of the river
and dashed off into a nearby field. When the horse's owner
found it, the *kappa* was still on its back. Together with the other
villagers, the owner tied the *kappa* up.

The villagers thought that the *kappa* should be killed for its
crimes, but the horse's owner had a different idea. 'No,' he said,

'we will not kill him. Instead, we will have him swear to never trouble us again.' The penitent *kappa* agreed, and he signed the document with his paw dipped in ink. After that, the villagers allowed the *kappa* to return to the river and, being a creature who keeps his word, he remained true to his promise and never bothered them again.

Amabie

In 2020 during the Covid-19 pandemic, a lesser-known *yōkai* experienced a popular resurgence. The *amabie* is a form of mer-creature with a beak-like mouth and three legs or fins. They fall into the category of *yogenjū*, prophecy creatures that appear to humans to make prophecies. The appearance of an *amabie* signals an abundant harvest followed by an epidemic, and making copies of its likeness will supposedly protect against illness.

BELOW: **This print of the *amabie* from a newspaper in the late Edo period is the earliest record of this *yōkai*.**

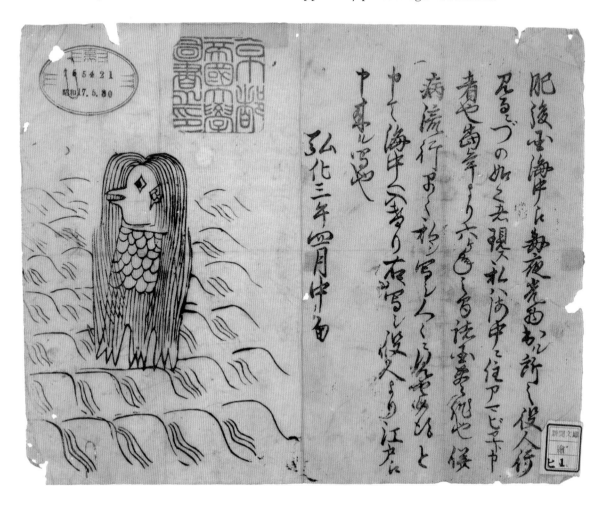

Tales of sightings spread from the 1840s onwards, with one of the first legends providing the template for following accounts. According to legend, an *amabie* first made its appearance in what is now Kumamoto Prefecture during May of 1846. A glowing object had been spotted in the sea night after night, so a local official went to investigate. There on the beach, he saw the *amabie*. Later, he made a sketch of it that showed long hair, a bird-like beak, three legs and a body covered in scales. The creature told the official that it was an *amabie* and that it lived out at sea. It had come to the land to deliver a prophecy: 'Good harvest will continue for six years from the current year; if disease spreads, draw a picture of me and show the picture of me to those who fall ill.' After that, it returned to the sea, and the official ensured that the tale and accompanying picture were printed and distributed in local woodblock-printed bulletins.

In early 2022, *amabie* images spread on the social media platform Twitter as a response to the Covid-19 pandemic, and the Ministry of Health, Labour and Welfare even used the *amabie*'s likeness on infection prevention posters.

Dragons

The Japanese term '*ryuu*' is generally translated into English as 'dragon', although the Japanese dragon is different to the fire-breathing creature of Western legends such as that of Saint George and the Dragon.

In Japan, dragons are usually water deities. They can be found as far back as in the *Kojiki* and the *Nihon Shoki*. Watatsumi the sea god is also the Dragon King, and Susano-wo slays the Yamata no Orochi, or eight-forked dragon.

They are depicted as long, serpentine creatures, an image that was introduced from China in ancient times. Many dragon-related terms and stories also came from China, such as the four Dragon Kings who rule over the North, South, East and West Seas. In fact, the diverse range of dragon-related stories found in Japanese mythology are often an amalgamation of native folklore and myths and stories imported from China, Korea and India, and the creature is associated with both Shinto and Buddhism. At Sensō-ji, the Buddhist temple in Asakusa dedicated to the

DRAGONS ARE DEPICTED AS LONG, SERPENTINE CREATURES, AN IMAGE THAT WAS INTRODUCED FROM CHINA IN ANCIENT TIMES.

RIGHT: Artisans making *shibu uchiwa* fans printed with *amabie* at Kurikawa Shoten in Kumamoto Prefecture.

RIGHT: Artisans making *shibu uchiwa* fans printed with *amabie* at Kurikawa Shoten in Kumamoto Prefecture.

bodhisattva Kannon, the Golden Dragon Dance has been performed bi-annually since 1958 to celebrate the reconstruction of the temple's main hall.

Dragons continued to be a popular motif into the modern era, associated with strength, power and fury. In World War II, armaments such as submarines and aircraft were often named after dragons. Dragon designs are also prevalent in the back and full-body tattoos favoured by members of the *yakuza* organized crime syndicate. One of the most famous Japanese manga and anime of all time, *Dragonball* is a long-running series that sees the protagonist going on adventures as he tries to collect seven orbs known as Dragon Balls, which can summon a wish-granting dragon.

Wani

Closely related to the dragon is the *wani*, a mythological sea creature that is something between a dragon, a crocodile and a shark. The *wani* appear in the *Kojiki* and the *Nihon Shoki* in the tales of the White Hare of Inaba and of Hoderi and his brother Hoori.

OPPOSITE: Ryūjin is often portrayed as a dragon. Print by Kuniyoshi Utagawa (1798–1861).

In the tale of Hoderi and Hoori in the first chapter, we left off after Hoderi had subjugated his brother; but the story did not end there. Hoderi's wife and daughter of the Owatatsumi was named Toyotama-hime. After Hoderi's brother had vowed to serve him, Toyotama-hime emerged from the sea to be with her husband. She was with child, and due to give birth soon. They built a birthing hut on the beach, and Toyotama-hime instructed Hoderi not to look upon her as she delivered the baby. However, as she went through the pains of labour, Hoderi became curious. He peeked into the hut and saw his wife transform into a crocodile-like creature. When Toyotama-hime realized that her husband had seen her in this state, she was deeply ashamed. She returned at once to the sea, leaving her newborn child behind.

Tsuchigumo

We previously encountered this spider-like creature in Emperor Jimmu's story. The name was originally a derogatory term for local clans who refused to obey the imperial court. The transition to a *yōkai* came in the medieval Kamakura period when *tsuchigumo* started to be depicted as giant *oni*-like spiders, their images growing more bizarre and frightening as the decades passed.

In *The Tale of Heike*, the epic account of the Genpei War compiled in the late Kamakura period, it is told how Minamoto no Yorimitsu slayed a giant spider and renamed his sword as Kumokiri, or Spider-Cutter. The story has been depicted in many other forms including a 15th-century Noh play *Tsuchigumo*, and a 14th-century picture scroll known as the *Tsuchigumo Sōshi*. The scroll also depicts many other *yōkai* such as a floating skull and possessed household utensils.

Raijū

With a name meaning 'thunder beast', *raijū* are mythological creatures whose bodies are made of lightning. They usually take the form of a white and blue wolf or dog, although they can also appear as any other kind of animal, or even simply a ball of lightning. They are a companion of Raijin, the Shinto god of lightning.

HE PEEKED INTO THE HUT AND SAW HIS WIFE TRANSFORM INTO A CROCODILE-LIKE CREATURE. WHEN TOYOTAMA-HIME EWALISED THAT HER HUSBAND HAD SEEN HER IN THIS STATE, SHE WAS DEEPLY ASHAMED.

Raijū are usually placid, but during thunderstorms they rampage around wildly, coming down to Earth on lightning bolts. The burns left on trees by lightning strikes are attributed to the *raijū's* claws. Interest in *raijū* declined after the Edo period as rapid developments in scientific knowledge during the Meiji era (1868– 1912) offered empirical explanations for the causes of lightning.

According to legend, a famous samurai of the Sengoku Warring States era (1477–1573), Tachibana Dōsetsu, was once struck by a bolt of lightning as he sought shelter from a storm under a tree. However, the warrior's quick reflexes allowed him to draw his sword and slice through the lightning and the *raijū* within. After this, he changed the name of his sword from Chidori, meaning 'thousand birds', to Raikiri, meaning Lightning-Cutter.

ABOVE: **The warrior Raikō battles a** *tsuchigumo* **in this print by Kuninaga Utagawa.**

Kitsune

The *kitsune* is hugely important to Japanese mythology and folklore. The word *kitsune* refers to all foxes, real and legendary. Folklore tells that all foxes have the ability to shapeshift into human form. Being seen as both cunning and charming has led to them being both feared and revered. The association with the Shinto *kami* Inari further contributed to the fox's mystical status.

The relationship between Japanese people and foxes can be traced back to the Neolithic Jōmon period (10,000–300 BCE) when people made necklaces from foxes' teeth and jaw bones. Later, Chinese tales of *huli jing* fox spirits melded with existing folklore.

BELOW: **Sculpture of a *kitsune* at Fushimi Inari Shrine in Kyoto.**

Foxes appear as supernatural beings in the *Nihon Shoki*, acting as messengers of omens both good and bad. The *Nihon Ryōiki* records the first written tale of a fox appearing as a woman and marrying a human man. These accounts of fox wives, or *kitsune-nyōbō*, were common even into the 20th century.

Kitsune are often portrayed as tricksters who possess women and swindle men. They can transform themselves into beautiful women, like Tamamo-no-Mae, in order to seduce men. As servants of Inari, foxes are guardian spirits and deities to be worshipped.

Nine-tailed fox

The concept of the nine-tailed fox, known as *kyūbi no kitsune* in Japanese, originated with the Chinese mythical creature, *huli jing*. China had its own rich tradition of fox tales, and in many the fox would assume the guise of a beautiful, seductive woman. The more tails a *kitsune* has, the older, wiser and more powerful it is.

The Pokémon Ninetails is based on the mythical nine-tailed fox and is called Kyukon in Japanese.

Komainu

Known as 'lion-dogs' in English, *komainu* are the guardian lions found standing in pairs at the entrance to Shinto shrines as well as temples or residences of wealthy families. Intended to ward off evil spirits, one of the pair usually has its mouth open while the other's

KYŌKAI'S FOX TALE

This early fox tale from the Nihon Ryōiki, a collection of Heian-period setsuwa written by the monk Kyōkai between the late 8th and early 9th century, is echoed in many other tales of fox-wives across the ages.

During the reign of Emperor Kinmei, a man from the Ouno district of Mino province set out on horseback in search of a good wife. In a field he came across a pretty and responsive girl. He winked at her and asked, 'Where are you going, Miss?' 'I am looking for a good husband,' she answered. So, he asked, 'Will you be my wife?' and, when she agreed, he took her to his house and married her.

Before long she became pregnant and gave birth to a boy. At the same time their dog also gave birth to a puppy, on the fifteenth of the twelfth month. This puppy barked constantly at the mistress and seemed fierce and ready to bite. She became so frightened that she asked her husband to beat the dog to death. But, he felt sorry for the dog and could not bear to kill it.

In the second or third month, when the annual quota of rice was hulled, she went to the place where the female servants were pounding rice in a mortar to provide refreshments. Seeing her, the dog ran after her barking and almost bit her. Startled and terrified, she suddenly changed into a wild fox and jumped up on top of the hedge.

Having seen this, the man said, 'Since a child was born between us, I cannot forget you. Please come always and sleep with me.' She acted in accordance with her husband's words and came and slept with him. For this reason, she was named 'Kitsune' meaning 'come and sleep'.

Slender and beautiful in her red skirt (it is called pink), she would rustle away from her husband, whereupon he sang of his love for his wife:

'Love fills me completely
After a moment of reunion.
Alas! She is gone.'

The man named his child Kitsune, which became the child's surname – Kitsune no atae. The child, famous for his enormous strength, could run as fast as a bird flies. He is the ancestor of the Kitsune-no-atae family in Mino province.

– Translation by Kyoko Motomachi Nakamura

RIGHT: *Surimono* print of a mirror with a nine-tailed fox design by Goshichi Harukawa (1776–1831), likely privately commissioned for the New Year.

is closed. This originates in Buddhist symbolism, where the open mouth pronounces the first letter of the Sanskrit alphabet and the closed mouth the last to form the sacred sound 'Aum'.

Shisa

The Ryukyuan *shisa* also derives from Chinese guardian lions, and they can be found in pairs on rooftops or guarding the gates to houses. The one on the left has its mouth closed to keep good spirits in, whereas the one on the right has its mouth open to ward off evil spirits.

Legend tells of how a Chinese emissary returned from a voyage to the court at Shuri Castle, a *gusuku* (castle) on the island of Okinawa, with a gift for the king. The gift was a necklace decorated with a *shisa* figurine, which the king took an instant liking to and wore every day.

One day, the king was visiting the village of Madanbashi on Naha Port bay. The village had recently been terrorized by a sea dragon that devoured villagers and destroyed homes. As the king was visiting, the sea dragon attacked. Terrified, the locals ran and hid. However, the local *noro* priest had previously been told in a dream to instruct the king to stand on the beach and lift up his figurine towards the dragon. She sent a messenger to inform him, and he did as she instructed.

The king faced the monster with the figurine held high, and immediately a giant roar resounded through the village, so deep and powerful that it even shook the dragon. Then, a massive boulder fell from Heaven and crushed the dragon's tail, pinning it in place until it eventually died.

Afterwards, the villagers built a large stone *shisa* to protect them from the dragon's spirit and other threats. Over time, plants covered the boulder and the dragon's body, and trees grew

BELOW: **A stone *shisa* stands guard at Shuri Castle in Okinawa.**

up around them. Today, this site is a small tree-covered mound known as Gaana-mui woods that can be found near Naha Ohashi bridge.

Cranes

In Japan, cranes, or *tsuru*, are said to live for a thousand years, making them symbols of good fortune and longevity. The red-crested crane is a common motif in art and can often be seen in the designs of luxurious silk kimono. In the Ainu language, the red-crowned crane is known as *sarurun kamuy* or 'marsh kamuy'. A popular folklore tale featuring a crane is *Tsuru no Ongaeshi*, or *The Grateful Crane*.

One day, a man saved a crane that had been shot down by hunters. Later that night, a beautiful woman appeared at the man's door and offered to be his wife. However, the man was very poor, and he told the woman that he wouldn't be able to support them both. Undeterred, the woman told him that she has a bottomless bag of rice, so she can keep them fed. The man welcomed her in.

The next day, the woman retired to her room, telling the man that she was going to make something and that he was not to enter the room until she was finished. After seven days, she emerged from the room with a beautiful piece of fabric she had woven, although the woman herself had become very thin.

The man took the cloth to market and was able to sell it for a handsome sum. Again, the woman said that she was retiring to her room to weave. This time, however, the man gave in to his curiosity and peeked into the room. There, he saw the woman transformed into a crane and realized that she was the very same crane he saved. When the crane saw that her husband had discovered her true identity, she flew away, never to return.

In the post-war period, the crane has become a symbol of peace thanks to a young girl named Sadako Sasaki. Sadako was only two years old when she survived the atomic bombing of Hiroshima. She went on to develop leukemia caused by radiation exposure. While she was in hospital, a friend told her of the legend of *senbazuru*, which tells how folding 1,000 origami paper cranes will grant the folder a wish. Inspired, Sadako set about

OPPOSITE: A formal kimono outer robe, called an *uchikake,* with an auspicious design featuring cranes, tortoises, chrysanthemums, plum blossoms, pine, and bamboo.

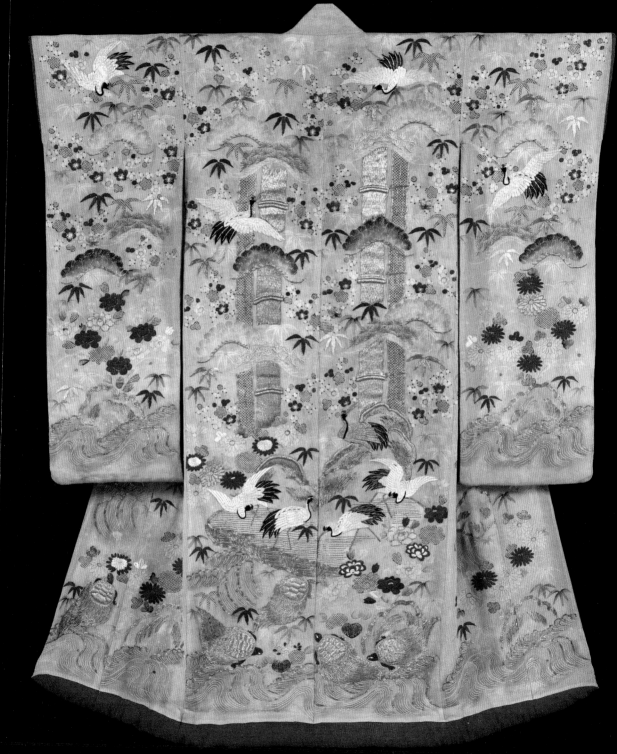

ABOVE: **The Children's Peace Monument at the Peace Memorial Park in Hiroshima uses the crane as a symbol of world peace.**

folding 1,000 cranes so that she could wish for a world without nuclear weapons, and she achieved her goal before she died in 1955 at the age of 12.

A statue of Sadako holding a golden crane called the Children's Peace Monument stands in the Hiroshima Peace Memorial Park. Paper cranes adorn the monument, donated by people from across the globe who share Sadako's wish for world peace.

Tanuki

Similar to *kitsune*, *tanuki* are real animals that also feature extensively in folklore. The *tanuki* is the Japanese raccoon dog (*Nyctereutes viverrinus*), a fluffy wild animal found throughout

Japan, from remote forests to diving through bins in urban areas. As a *yōkai*, they are called *bake-danuki*. They are mischievous shapeshifters, often using their powers to make fools of people. They appear in texts as far back as the *Nihon Shoki* and the *Nihon Ryōiki*. There is a distinctly comical aspect to the *tanuki*; they are often depicted as having extremely oversized testicles that they sometimes fling over their backs. A playground chant goes as follows:

> *Tan-tan-tanuki's bollocks,*
> *Even without wind,*
> *They swiiing-swing!*

BELOW: Tanuki statues are especially common in the Kansai region and are often cute or comical.

Statues of *tanuki* can be found all over Japan, often with large pot bellies, wearing a straw hat and holding bottles of sake (with or without the oversized testicles). There is a particular concentration in Shiga Prefecture, which is famous for its *tanuki* pottery.

Kirin

The *kirin* originates from the Chinese *qilin*, a hooved, chimera-like creature said to appear with the coming or passing of an eminent sage or ruler; the birth and death of Confucius were supposedly heralded by *qilin*. The Japanese *kirin* resembles a deer with dragon-like scales covering its body and the tail of an ox. It has a flowing, fiery mane and a serene expression. It is considered to be a gentle, sacred animal. *Kirin* may have one or two horns, and they are associated with the Western unicorn due to their similarities.

Kirin is also the word for giraffe. This originates from when the Chinese explorer Zheng He brought back exotic creatures from his expedition to Africa in the early 15th

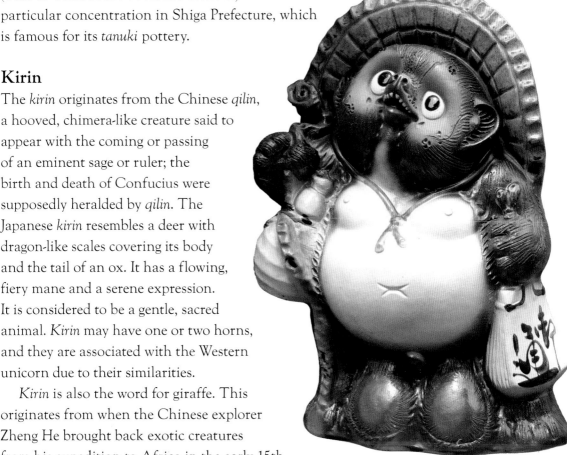

THE *TANUKI*-KETTLE

The story of *Bunbuku Chagama* features both a creature and an object: a *tanuki* and a teapot. It became popular during the Edo and Meiji periods in woodblock-printed illustrated literature called *kusazōshi*.

At the temple of Morin-ji in present-day Gunma Prefecture, the head priest owned a *chagama* tea kettle. One day, when he went to put it on the hearth, the kettle sprouted the head, legs and tail of a *tanuki*. The half-tanuki/half-kettle proceeded to dance wildly around the room until the priest and his novices were eventually able to catch it.

With the kettle returned to an ordinary kettle form, the priest sold it on to a travelling tinker. That night, the tinker was awoken by a strange noise to find that his newly purchased kettle had transformed into a *tanuki*.

When he told his friends about this bizarre occurrence, they told him that he should be pleased as he had a moneymaker on his hands. They advised him to tour the country with the *tanuki*-kettle, putting on shows where it would do tricks and walk the tightrope. The tinker heeded this advice and worked out a deal with the *tanuki*, promising to look after it and to never to put the kettle over a hot flame.

After the tinker had become a wealthy man, he returned the kettle to the temple where it was kept as an object of worship.

An ink painting of the tanuki who turned into a tea kettle by Kyōsai Kawanabe (1831–1889).

century. This included a giraffe which was, at the time, believed to be a real-life *qilin*. The *kirin* also features as the logo for Kirin Beer, which has been brewed in Japan since 1888.

Mukade

Mukade are another real creature, this time from the insect family – the centipede. They are a familiar, if unwelcome, sight in Japan where they infest houses and terrify families due to their size, growing up to 20cm (8in), as well as their poisonous secretions and vicious bite.

They also feature as *yōkai*, particularly as *ōmukade*, or giant centipedes. These are big enough to eat a human being whole but are known to have a weakness to saliva. The most famous example appears in the *Tale of Tawara Tōda*, a heroic account of the legendary exploits of Fujiwara no Hidesato, a court noble and warrior of the Heian period. The story became popular in the Edo period when it was circulated via *emaki* picture scrolls and wood-block printed *otogi-zōshi* books.

One day on his travels, Fujiwara no Hidesato came to a bridge that spanned Lake Biwa. When he went to cross the bridge, he found a great coiled serpent blocking the way. Undeterred, Hidesato stepped lightly across the creature's back and went on his way.

After he had crossed the bridge, Hidesato heard someone call to him. Turning around, he found a man (in some versions of the story it is a young woman who is the Sea King's daughter) who proclaimed that he was the Dragon King of the sea. He had transformed himself into the terrifying serpent in order to find a brave mortal who was not afraid of him. The Dragon King told Hidesato of how a great centipede had been terrorizing the area, devouring animals and people alike, and that he was seeking a warrior who could defeat the beast.

ABOVE: **This *kirin* carving has a single horn. The mythological creature originates with the Chinese *quilin* and is similar to a chimera.**

ABOVE: **Hidesato battles a giant centipede. Print by Shuntei Katsukawa (1762–1819).**

Brave warrior that he was, Hidesato agreed to help. When he came to Mount Mikami he saw that the great centipede had wound itself around the mountain, its thousands of legs glowing like a procession of lanterns across the dark hills.

A skilled marksman, Hidesato drew his bow and shot an arrow. It hit the centipede in the head but glanced straight off. Again, he shot, and again the arrow glanced off harmlessly. With his third and last arrow, he coated it with his own saliva and prayed to his patron Hachiman. The arrow flew straight and true, and this time it pierced through the creature's skull, killing it.

The Dragon King took Hidesato down to his palace beneath the waves and threw a grand feast for him. He also gave him precious gifts: a never-ending bolt of silk, a copper pan of plenty and an inexhaustible bag of rice. It was for this rice bag that he received the nickname Tawara Tōda, with '*tawara*' meaning 'rice bag'. There is a small shrine dedicated to Hidesato near to the Seta Bridge at Lake Biwa.

Kijimuna

In Okinawan mythology, *kijimuna* are wood sprites. These small, childlike creatures have large heads from which sprouts wild, bright red hair, and they make their home in the banyan trees native to the tropical island. Modern versions tend to depict *kijimuna* as more human and elflike than older descriptions of furred creatures that can blend in with the trees. As well as being excellent fishers, they are very mischievous and love to play tricks on humans.

Mintuci

The *mintuci kamuy* is a water sprite from Ainu mythology, similar to the *kappa*. They are small, humanoid creatures with purple or red skin, said to be half-human half-animal, sometimes with bird-like feet or hooves. Like the *kappa*, they will drag livestock and people underwater with them. They can also possess people, and a woman possessed by a *mintuci* may attempt to seduce men. The *mintuci* may also help people, albeit for a price; the cost of a local *mintuci* ensuring a bountiful catch of fish from its waters is an increase in drownings.

Bears

As the largest native land predator, the bear was a particularly important animal to the Ainu and was considered the 'clothing' of the mountain god Nuparikor Kamuy.

The Ainu engaged in a bear ritual up until the early 20th century. A bear cub would be raised for a year before being shot dead with arrows and displayed for a week while people gave it offerings of wine, song and dance. After this, the deity inhabiting the bear was sent back to its homeland, while its 'clothing' was left behind in the form of its fur and flesh to be enjoyed by the people. Bears that were not given the proper rituals and offerings became monstrous and were then called *ararush*. They could attack people, dam up rivers and scare off other animals.

Daruma

The *daruma* doll itself is not considered mythological, but it is an object steeped in myth and symbolism. The Buddhist monk Bodhidharma lived around the 5th or 6th century CE and is credited with introducing Cha'an, or Zen Buddhism, to China. He features in various legends, many of which revolve around his meditation practices. One tells that he sat facing a wall for

THE DRAGON KING TOOK HIDESATO DOWN TO HIS PALACE BENEATH THE WAVES AND THREW A GRAND FEAST FOR HIM. HE ALSO GAVE HIM PRECIOUS GIFTS: A NEVER-ENDING BOLT OF SILK, A COPPER PAN OF PLENTY AND AN INEXHAUSTIBLE BAG OF RICE.

nine years, causing his arms and legs to atrophy and drop off. Another says that he fell asleep during this nine-year meditation, and afterwards he was so angry at himself that he cut off his own eyelids to prevent it from happening again. He is portrayed as wide-eyed and wild-bearded.

The *daruma* as a talisman originates with the Zen Buddhist Shorinzan Daruma Temple in Gunma Prefecture. The founding myth of the temple tells how in the late 17th century the Usui River flooded from heavy rains. Afterwards, the villagers found a glowing tree near the riverbed. Declaring it sacred, they placed it inside a hut with the local Kannon statue; as they did so, a purple haze filled the air.

Around the same time, Bodhidharma appeared in a dream to the travelling monk, Ichiryo Koji. He commanded Koji to carve his likeness out of a tree that was exactly the height of his nose. Koji began searching for such a tree and eventually found it when he visited the village that had been flooded. He carefully carved the Bodhidharma's likeness then placed it beside the Kannon statue, enshrining them together. The local villagers were inspired by Ichiryo Koji's devotion, and after the temple was founded, there began a custom of visitors receiving charms depicting

BELOW: **The *iomante* ritual performed by the Ainu people involved sacrificing and "sending off" the spirit of a bear.**

Bodhidharma for luck at New Year's. Today, the temple holds an annual Daruma Doll Festival, and many of the country's *daruma* dolls are produced in the area.

The *daruma* doll is generally a round doll made from papier-mâché. It is hollow but weighted at the bottom like a wobble toy. Its body is red with gold designs, it has black facial hair and the eyes are blank. After purchasing a *daruma*, the owner fills in one eye with a black pupil while setting a goal then fills in the other once their goal is complete. *Daruma* are traditionally burned at the end of the year at the temple where they were purchased in a ceremony called *daruma kuyō*.

Tsukumogami

Tsukumogami are objects, often tools, that have acquired a spirit. In general, this is considered to happen when an object reaches 100 years of age. They feature in many *emakimono* from the Muromachi period, such as the *Tsukumogami Emaki* and the *Hyakki Yagyō Emaki* and in Edo-period *ukiyo-e* woodblock prints.

ABOVE: **Daruma dolls are burned in an annual ceremony at the end of the year.**

Some *tsukumogami* have their own names, for example, *boroboroton*, or 'tattered futon', is a *tsukumogami yōkai* in the form of a futon. It comes to life at night and wraps itself around the neck of any sleeping people in the house to strangle them, usually due to feeling ignored or unwanted. Sometimes, it simply meets with other *tsukumogami* to throw a noisy party.

The *kasa-obake* is an old umbrella that comes to life with one eye and jumps around on one leg. There are no specific folklore

RIGHT: A print of a one-legged umbrella yōkai by Gosōtei Hirosada.

tales about them, so they are generally thought to be a *yōkai* that originated from made-up illustrations, like a manga character.

Ittan-momen is a *yōkai* that takes the form of a piece of cloth, sometimes with arms and legs, that flutters around and attacks people by wrapping around their faces and suffocating them. They were popularized with the 1960 manga *GeGeGe no Kitarō* by Shigeru Mizuki, perhaps leading to some of the supposed present-day sightings.

Kaiju

It may seem strange to include *kaiju* among this list of mythological creatures; after all, they are a fictional creation, and no one truly believes they exist, except perhaps for very small children. However, they have become a part of modern mythology – not myths in the traditional sense, but fulfilling a similar cultural role.

In the early 20th century, the term *kaiju*, which literally translates as 'strange beast', was used to refer to the cryptids that captured imagination around the world, but it was as the stars of monster movies that the name really gained prominence. *Kaiji* is now the term for giant monsters that rampage through Japan and sometimes the world on film, stomping over cities and battling one another. The most famous of all *kaiju* is Godzilla, a legendary movie monster that has appeared in multi-million-dollar Hollywood movies.

In 1954, Ishirō Honda's *Gojira* took Japan by storm. Yet *Gojira* was more than just a monster movie; it was an allegory for the destruction wrought on Japan by the dropping of nuclear bombs on Hiroshima and Nagasaki at the end of the Pacific War. Godzilla was an unstoppable force wreaking destruction through the film's Tokyo, and the director stated that 'If Godzilla had been a dinosaur or some other animal, he would have been killed by just one cannonball. But if he were equal to an atomic bomb, we wouldn't know what to do. So, I took the characteristics of an atomic bomb and applied them to Godzilla.'

In the 2016 film *Shin Gojira*, Godzilla collectively represented the destruction of the 2011 Tōhoku earthquake and tsunami and the Fukushima Daiichi nuclear disaster. The film depicted the

THE MOST FAMOUS OF ALL *KAIJU* IS GODZILLA, A LEGENDARY MOVIE MONSTER THAT HAS APPEARED IN MULTI-MILLION-DOLLAR HOLLYWOOD MOVIES.

水爆大怪獣映画

ゴジラ

原作 香山 滋
脚本 村田武雄
本多猪四郎

ABOVE: Poster for the
original Godzilla movie
from 1954.

Japanese bureaucracy's slow response in the face of crisis.

Yōkai in the modern age

As previously shown, there has always been a domestic (later global) audience for stories and artwork depicting Japan's mythological creatures. In the modern era, *yōkai* have become more commercialized than ever.

Playing cards were introduced to Japan by Portuguese traders, and Japanese versions called *karuta* started to be developed towards the end of the 16th century. Illustrated cards used to play picture-matching games were called *e-awase karuta*, and there are many different variant decks featuring all kinds of imagery. The *Obake Karuta* was a deck created in the Edo period that remained popular until the 1920s, with each card featuring a creature from Japanese mythology. It can be seen as a precursor to modern trading cards games like Yu-Gi-Oh! and the Pokémon Trading Card Game; in fact, many Pokémon are also based on *yōkai*.

In 1960, the manga series *GeGeGe no Kitarō*, created by Shigeru Mizuki, further popularized *yōkai* in a modern form. It follows Kitarō, a *yōkai* boy with supernatural powers who works to unite the worlds of humans and *yōkai*. On his adventures, he befriends and fights against an assortment of different *yōkai*. As well as *yōkai* folklore, the series references other traditional tales such as Momotarō.

Building on the enduring popularity of *yōkai* as collectible companions, Yo-kai Watch is a multimedia franchise that originated with a video game in 2013. The series revolves around befriending 'Yo-kai', cartoonish creatures based on traditional *yōkai*. It is hugely popular with children in Japan, and the game series and anime have enjoyed international success.

Yōkai have long held a fascination for Japanese people, and even with the science and scepticism of the modern era, that has not changed, although the way in which people interact with the concept has. To many people, *yōkai* have shed their fearsome pasts and become cuddly critters beloved by children; on the other hand, they also remain a staple of the horror genre. Either way, Japan's native mythological creatures are still part of daily life through their prominence in entertainment, and they provide a shared cultural imagery that is as societally ingrained as the ancient *kami* and legendary heroes. While genuine belief in the creatures discussed here may have faded, modern Japan has no shortage of other spirits and spooks that still send a shiver down people's spines.

BELOW: **Mizuki Shigeru Road in Tottori Prefecture featured sculptures of yōkai from the manga author's famous series** *Gegege no Kitaro.*

5

GHOSTS AND URBAN LEGENDS

Vengeful spirits have always been a part of Japanese folklore as far back as the legendary emperors in the *Kojiki*, and the introduction of Buddhism brought with it its own cadre of spooks and spectres. While ghosts have always been considered a form of *yōkai*, in the modern era they are generally viewed as their own distinct category, and most modern urban legends centre around ghosts, or *yūrei*, rather than *yōkai*.

Legends surrounding ghosts are intrinsically linked to the telling of ghost stories, which has been a popular pastime for centuries and has always blurred the lines between purportedly true tales and fiction. With advances in printing technology during the Edo period (1603–1868), the demand for collections of spooky tales soared, and popular games such as the *hyakumonogatari kaidankai* fuelled people's interest in stories of the supernatural. As communication became faster and more accessible, local predominantly oral folklore had the potential to be disseminated on a national scale, and it was during this era that many of

OPPOSITE: **Japanese folklore is filled with an assortment of ghosts, goblins, and ghouls.**

RIGHT: **The Ghost of Koheiji Kohada, from Hokusai's print series** *One Hundred Ghost Tales.*

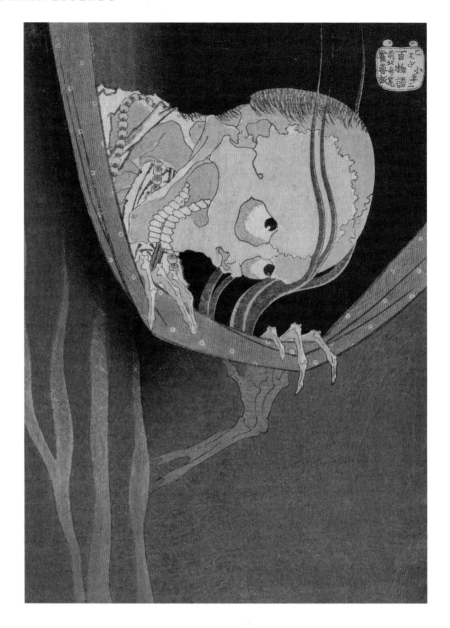

the characteristics that would later become staples of modern Japanese horror were codified.

Similarly, other technological advances have also led to booms in occult interest. In the 1970s, mass media contributed to an interest in and fear of various urban legends, particularly the way they spread among school-age children, which bears some similarity to the Satanic panic of the 1980s in the United States. The arrival of the internet in the late 1990s saw another explosion in urban legends and accompanying fear; instant communication facilitated new types of storytelling, and the unknown expanses of the World Wide Web provided fertile grounds for the development of what came to be termed 'netlore'. As technology continues to evolve, Japan's ghosts and ghouls will no doubt continue to adapt alongside it.

Hyakumonogatari Kaidankai

This parlour game was inspired by Buddhist didactic storytelling. While its origins are unclear, it likely started in the early Edo period among the samurai class.

To play this '100 ghost story gathering', a group of people gather together at nightfall. In another room, 100 *andon* lanterns or candles are lit and a small mirror placed on a table. Then, the guests take turns telling scary stories, with a particular emphasis on those that are purported to be true. These stories are called *kaidan* or 'strange narratives'. At the end of each story, the teller goes into the other room, extinguishes one lamp, and looks into the mirror before rejoining the group. As the session progresses, the room grows darker and darker until the 100th tale is reached, at which point the atmosphere is perfect for the evocation of a spirit; in fact, the game itself serves as a ritual to summon supernatural beings. However, most sessions stop at the 99th tale for fear of completing the ritual.

During the Edo period, the game quickly grew in popularity and spread among the working class, leading to greater demand for spooky folk tales that could be told during the game. This was also when the traditional modern image of the *yūrei* was solidified. New printing technology led to a boom in book publication, and *kaidan* collections proved to be a big hit. The *Shokoku Hyakumonogatari* (*100 Tales of Many Countries*) featured supposedly true supernatural stories from around the world, and since then the term *hyakumonogatari* has often been used in titles of books in the same genre.

Although the popularity of the game itself has faded, it has had a lasting impact. Telling ghost stories is still a popular pastime among schoolchildren, particularly young girls, during the summer months. It has also influenced the Japanese horror genre and the style in which urban legends are told.

ABOVE: A scene from the film *One Hundred Ghost Stories* showing Rokurokubi, a yōkai with a long, stretchy neck.

OPPOSITE: The Ghost of Oyuki is a painting of a female yūrei by Ōkyo Maruyama (1733–1795). He painted it after the spirit of his dead mistress came to him in a dream.

Yūrei

The umbrella term for all types of ghost is *yūrei*. They are spirits of the dead who have been denied a peaceful afterlife, similar to the Western concept of ghosts. Usually, a person's spirit joins its ancestors in the afterlife, only returning to the land of the living during the annual festival of Obon in August. However, if a person dies violently, if the proper rites are not performed or if they harbour intense emotions such as love, desire for revenge, sorrow, jealousy or hatred, the spirit can become a *yūrei*. The *yūrei* may be laid to rest by performing the correct rituals or by resolving its emotional conflict. Japanese ghosts are myriad, and there are specific terms for some of the most common types, which we will discuss later.

In 1750, Maruyama Ōkyo painted *The Ghost of Oyuki*, which is the earliest known artwork showing the style of *yūrei* that would become the archetype that persists to the present day. The *yūrei* is typically dressed in white, evoking the white burial kimono used in Edo funeral rites, and has long, dishevelled black hair. It has dangling hands and floats across the ground without feet or legs. While this has been a recognizable figure to Japanese people for centuries, it is now also identifiable worldwide, mostly thanks to the 1998 Japanese horror film franchise *Ringu* or *The Ring*. In it, Sadako Yamamura, a young woman who was killed by being thrown down a well, comes back as a vengeful spirit thanks to a cursed video tape. The image of her crawling out of a television, her long black hair covering her face, has sent shivers down many a spine; it also exemplifies how traditional *yūrei* lore has evolved to embrace new technology.

Gakki

These spirits are specific to Buddhism and may be called 'hungry ghosts' in English. As punishment for their mortal vices, the spirits of greedy or jealous people are cursed with an insatiable hunger for a particular thing and are cursed to wander the earth,

forever seeking but never satisfied. Some are cursed to seek out human flesh, and these are called *jikininki*. They come out at night to scavenge for fresh corpses and loot offerings left for the dead.

The *Ugetsu Monogatari* (*Tales of Moonlight and Rain*) was published by Ueda Akinari in 1776. It contains nine supernatural stories that have been adapted from traditional Japanese and Chinese ghost stories. One of these – 'Aozuki' ('The Blue Hood') – follows the tradition of Buddhist *setsuwa* stories.

In it, a travelling Buddhist monk visits a village where he learns that the local priest has become a cannibalistic demon. The man had gone insane following the death of his young male lover, and subsequently ate the flesh of the corpse. The monk confronts the demon, which has been terrorizing the village, and places a blue priest's hood over its head to provide religious salvation.

Onryō

An *onryō* is a vengeful spirit that can hurt or kill people and even cause natural disasters as it seeks to exact vengeance for the wrongs it endured when alive. They have long been a part of traditional Japanese beliefs, and many famous examples of *yūrei* fall within this category.

The native belief in *onryō* has been around since ancient times; Emperor Sutoku, Taira no Masakado and Sugawara Michizane (Tenjin) are known as the Three Great Onryō. After these great men died, their resentment and anger brought them back as spirits and they wreaked vengeance with wars, natural disasters and plagues. Eventually, each was enshrined as a *kami* and deified in a Shinto shrine to appease them. They are also referred to as *goyō*, a term for a noble or accomplished person who died prematurely and came back to bring disaster to those who wronged them before becoming a *kami*.

Taira no Masakado's burial mound now sits on a prime piece of real estate in central Tokyo, surrounded by skyscrapers. There have been various attempts during the 20th century to move the headstone, but each was apparently thwarted by a spate of bad luck, leading to the memorial being left to reside there permanently in a tiny garden.

AN ONRYŌ IS
A VENGEFUL
SPIRIT THAT CAN
HURT OR KILL
PEOPLE AND EVEN
CAUSE NATURAL
DISASTERS AS IT
SEEKS TO EXACT
VENGEANCE FOR
THE WRONGS IT
ENDURED WHEN
ALIVE.

Hōsōshin

Also known as *hōsōgami*, the *hōsōshin* is a smallpox demon. When smallpox was introduced to Japan, it was believed to be caused by *onryō*, and people attempted to assuage it to cure the infection. Smallpox demons are supposedly afraid of red things and dogs. In Okinawa, musical performances on the *sanshin* stringed instrument and lion dances by people wearing red were performed to try to pacify the smallpox demon. People also wrote collections of traditional *ryūka* poetry in the Ryūkyūan language that was designed to appease it.

Banchō Sarayashiki

Banchō Sarayashiki is a traditional ghost story about an *onryō*. Although it first officially appeared as a *bunraku* puppet play in

ABOVE: **Taira no Masakado's tomb stands on some of the most expensive land in the world in Tokyo's financial district.**

1741, folk versions of the tale existed well before then, with many regional variations.

There was once a beautiful servant by the name of Okiku who worked for a samurai. The samurai would often tell Okiku that he was in love with her and wanted to marry her, but she always refused his advances. Eventually, he grew tired of this and decided to force her hand. He tricked Okiku into believing that she had carelessly lost one of the family's ten precious pottery plates, a crime worthy of death. Distraught, she counted the plates again and again, but there were only nine, and she had no idea where the tenth could be. She went to the samurai to beg for forgiveness, and he agreed to pardon her if she would marry him – but again, she refused. This sent

ABOVE: **Minamoto no Tametomo drives away demons in this print by Yoshitoshi Tsukioka (1839–1892), part of his *Thirty-six Ghosts* series.**

the samurai into a rage, and he threw Okiku down a well, killing her. After this, Okiku came back as an *onryō* and haunted her tormentor by counting to nine over and over again and letting out a bloodcurdling shriek in place of the number ten.

Another famous version of the story was written by Okamoto Kido and appeared in 1916. In this retelling, it becomes a tragic romance, signalling the changing tastes of theatre-going audiences.

Yotsuya Kaidan

This tale started life as a kabuki play in 1825, first appearing as a double-feature with *Kanadehon Chūshingura*, and has subsequently been adapted and retold countless times, becoming one of Japan's best-known ghost stories. Featuring a large cast of characters, the plot is long and involved and cannot be recounted in full here, but the story revolves around a *rōnin* named Tamiya Iemon and his love interest Oiwa.

Iemon becomes enraged when Oiwa's father suggests the couple should not be together, and kills him. He hides his crime from Oiwa and convinces her that he will find and exact revenge upon the culprit. Meanwhile, another woman, Oume, has fallen in love with Iemon. Jealous of Oiwa's beauty, Oume arranges for Oiwa to be sent a facial cream laced with poison that disfigures her pretty face. When Iemon sees his wife's ghastly countenance, he is repulsed and decides that he can no longer be with her. He tries to get a friend to rape her so that he has grounds for divorce, but instead the man simply shows Oiwa her own face in a mirror. In her distress, she ends up stabbing herself through the throat. As she lies bleeding to death, she curses Iemon.

Not long after Oiwa's death, Iemon becomes engaged to Oume, but on their wedding night he is tricked into killing his new bride by Oiwa's ghost. He also kills Oume's grandfather and then her mother. Haunted by Oiwa's ghost, he flees to an isolated mountain where he descends into madness as Oiwa continues to haunt him. Eventually, he is killed by another character out of both vengeance and compassion.

BELOW: **Okiku came back as an *onryō* to haunt the samurai master who made her miserable during life.**

The ghost of Oiwa is an *onryō* whose desire for revenge brings her back to the earthly realm. She is depicted with the classic ghostly characteristics of long ragged hair, white dress and deathly pale skin. She also has a drooping left eye due to the disfiguring effects of the poisoned facial cream.

The play was a huge hit with audiences who couldn't get enough of its brutal, tragic violence and themes of revenge, and it continues to be popular today.

Candy Ghost

Stories of ghostly mothers buying sweets for their children have been around for a surprisingly long time. The folk tale may originate in China where a similar tale is recorded in the *Yijian Zhi*, a 420-chapter story collection completed in 1161. The candy shops in the stories are usually located at the top of a slope, perhaps due to an association with Yomotsu Hirasaka, a slope that appears in the *Kojiki* and acts as the boundary between the land of the living and Yomi, the land of the dead. These stories were used as didactic tales by Buddhist monks to preach about parental obligations and filial piety. One such story takes place in Okinawa on a slope called Nanachibaka (Seven Tomb Slope).

Once, there was a small candy shop near the forest at the top of Nanachibaka. One day, a woman appeared in the area and proceeded to come to the shop every night to buy candy. However, by the next morning, the money she used to pay for the sweets would turn into the joss paper that was burned as offerings to the dead, known as *uchikabi* in Okinawa.

Finding this curious, one night the shop owner followed the woman after she had purchased her sweets and left. The woman entered the forest and went to one of the tombs, which she entered. The shop owner followed her inside. To their shock, they found the decaying corpse of a young woman. Beside her sat a healthy, living baby, happily munching on candy.

Ghostly Lights

There are many different 'atmospheric ghost lights' that people claim to have seen across Japan. *Onibi* – literally translated as 'demon fire' – are supposedly spirits that have risen from the

OPPOSITE: Iemon is confronted by the spirit of his murdered wife, Oiwa, which appears in a broken lantern. Part of Hokusai's *One Hundred Ghost Stories* print series.

ABOVE: A print by
Chikanobu Toyohara
(1838–1912) of a scene
where *kitsunebi* appear
in the kabuki play
Honchō Nijūshikō.

corpses of dead people and animals. Published in 1712, the *Wakan Sansai Zue (Illustrated Sino-Japanese Encyclopedia)* described them as a blue light that floated above the ground.

Kitsunebi are another kind of ghost light, or 'fox fire', that appear in a line of ten to hundreds, flickering like lantern lights. They are generally red or orange in colour. Like the *kitsune*, they trick humans, usually by leading them off the road and into the mountains, similar to a will-o'-the-wisp. *Hitodama* (literally meaning 'human soul') are very similar to *onibi* and *kitsunebi*, but they are the souls of the dead that have left their bodies and now float through the night.

Today such phenomena can be attributed to scientific explanations such as light refraction, ball lightning or natural gas combustion. The *shiranui* is a phenomenon observed over the open waters of the Yatsushiro Sea and the Ariake Sea around Kyushu, which has been recorded as far back as in the *Nihon Shoki*. Flames would appear over the water then multiply until there were hundreds or thousands, spanning for several kilometres. Originally, locals believed them to be the lamps of the Dragon God, but studies in the 20th century have since concluded that they are the result of an atmospheric optical phenomenon. However, there are many other similar sightings from around the country that have yet to be explained.

Lafcadio Hearn

Born on the Greek island of Lefkada in 1850, Lafcadio Hearn went on to become the most influential popular scholar of Japanese culture in the 20th century. Following periods in Ireland, the United States and the West Indies while he developed his career as a reporter, Hearn moved to Japan in 1890. After becoming acquainted with Basil Hall Chamberlain, he began to teach and started work on various translation and book projects. He married a Japanese woman, Setsuko Koizumi, who was his collaborator on his translations, and became a Japanese citizen with the legal name Koizumi Yakumo. He died in Tokyo in 1904.

When Hearn moved there, Japan had only recently opened its borders to the world following the Meiji Restoration of 1868, and his English-language works were some of the first to introduce Japanese culture and history to foreign audiences. His story and essay collections were highly influential in the West where *Japonisme* was in vogue and Japanese art and aesthetics were becoming extremely fashionable.

Hearn was also hugely popular in Japan, and his former residence next to the Lafcadio Hearn Memorial Museum in Matsue are still popular tourist destinations. His English writings were translated into Japanese, resulting in a fascinating cross-cultural exchange whereby a Western man's interpretations of Japanese folk tales were reabsorbed back into the Japanese canon.

One of Hearn's most influential publications, *Glimpses of Unfamiliar Japan* (1894), collects travel writings from his early days in Japan together with discussions about the native culture, religion and people including local folklore. However, *Kwaidan: Stories and Studies of Strange Things* (1904) is probably his most famous work – a collection of Japanese ghost stories that has captured readers' imaginations around the world. Translated into Japanese, the collection is considered a classic in Japan. The 1964 Japanese anthology horror film *Kwaidan*, directed by

KITSUNEBI ARE ANOTHER KIND OF GHOST LIGHT, OR 'FOX FIRE', THAT APPEAR IN A LINE OF TEN TO HUNFREDS, FLICKERING LIKE LANTERN LIGHTS... LIKE THE *KITSUNE*, THEY TRICK HUMANS, USUALLY BY LEADING THEM OFF THE ROAD AND INTO THE MOUNTAINS.

Masaki Kobayashi, is based on Hearn's stories, and it received an Academy Award nomination for Best Foreign Language Film.

In modern times, Hearn's works have been criticized for exoticizing his subject and portraying a biased image of Japan. To him, Japan was a mysterious and unique land, and he placed great emphasis on characteristics he perceived as distinctly 'Oriental'. On the other hand, it could be said that Hearn's enduring popularity in Japan is due to his positive presentation of Japan and his assertion as an outsider of the country's unique native identity.

BELOW: **Lafcadio Hearn (1850–1904) was born in Greece but later settled in Japan where he took the name Yakumo Koizumi.**

Yuki-onna

There is evidence that stories of *yuki-onna* (the 'snow woman') have existed since at least the Muromachi era (1338–1477) and different regions of Japan have their own versions of the legend. All feature a ghostly woman who appears on snowy nights – she is tall and beautiful with long black hair, icy blue lips and deathly pale skin. She may be completely nude or wear a white kimono to blend in with the snow. The figure floats across the snowy ground leaving no footprints and strikes fear into the hearts of those who glimpse her.

There are many regional variations recorded by Japanese folklorists, but the version that most Japanese people are familiar with today was originally written in English then translated into Japanese. Lafcadio Hearn's *The Snow Bride*, published in his 1904 work *Kwaidan: Stories and Studies of Strange Things*, not only popularized the story for English-speaking audiences

"ONE OF THE YEAR'S 10 BEST!"
— Bosley Crowther, N.Y. Times
— Saturday Review

Walter Reade-Sterling proudly presents

KWAIDAN

directed by Masaki Kobayashi
screenplay by Yoko Mizuki
music by Toru Takemitsu
photographed by Yoshio Miyajima
EASTMANCOLOR · Filmed in TOHOSCOPE
CONTINENTAL

ABOVE: Poster for the Japanese movie *Kwaidan,* which was based on a collection of translated Japanese ghost stories by Lafcadio Hearn.

but influenced future Japanese interpretations. Indeed, Tokuzō Tanaka's 1968 film *The Snow Woman* adapted and expanded on Hearn's retelling.

Long ago, there lived two woodcutters. Their names were Minokichi, who was young, and Mosaku, who was old. One day, they found themselves in a snowstorm and sought shelter in a small hut. Mosaku fell asleep almost at once whereas Minokichi lay awake listening to the wail of the wind. Eventually he too slept, until he was awakened by the icy chill of snow. He saw that the door to the hut stood open and a beautiful pale woman dressed in pure white had entered the room. As he watched, the woman bent over the sleeping Mosaku and sighed a breath of white mist over him.

As Minokichi lay there, frozen in fear, the woman turned and approached him. Then she stopped and said to him, 'I was going

RIGHT: **Yuki-onna from a scroll illustrating thirty-five famous ghosts of Japan by an unknown artist.**

OPPOSITE: **Poster for a 1968 film, *The Snow Woman,* which expands upon Lafcadio Hearn's Yuki-onna story in his *Kwaidan* ghost story collection.**

to kill you, too, but you are too young and handsome to die. I will let you live, but you must tell no one about this incident. If you do, I will kill you.'

The woman then vanished into thin air. Minokichi tried to rouse the older man, but found him dead, his body as cold as ice.

The next winter, Minokichi encountered a pretty young woman by the name of Yuki (a common name, but also the Japanese word for 'snow'). He immediately fell in love with her, and the two were soon married. They had a happy life together and were blessed with many healthy children. The only strange thing was that Yuki never seemed to age and her beauty never diminished.

One night, after the children were in bed, Minokichi was looking at his wife when a memory came back to him. He said to his wife, 'Yuki, you remind me so much of a beautiful woman I once saw when I was young. She killed my friend with her ice-cold breath. I do not know if she was a dream or a spectre, but tonight I seem to see her in you.'

On hearing this, Yuki got to her feet, a horrible smile twisting her lips. 'It was I who you met back then, and I who killed your friend. I told you that I would kill you should you tell anyone, and now you have broken that promise; were it not for our children, you would already be dead. Take care of them, and see that you do, otherwise I *will* return when the snow next falls and kill you.'

Then, with a hideous shriek, she turned into a cloud of white mist and blew out of the house, never to be seen again.

Black Hair

Together with long, black hair being a feature of many *yūrei*, hair itself plays a part in many ghost stories and urban legends. Hair had great significance in aristocratic women's lives from the Heian period (794–1192) onwards, with many hours dedicated to haircare and styling. Stemming from this preoccupation, there were many hair-related legends and *yōkai*; for example, the *kamikiri* was a small creature with a scissor-like beak and pincers for hands that would sneak into houses and cut people's hair off while they slept.

The imagery of long, black, dishevelled hair became associated with the *yūrei* during the Edo period, and its ghostly associations have continued to the present day; we see Sadako brushing her hair before the mirror in the Japanese horror film *The Ring*, and black hair coming out of a tap in the 2002 film *Dark Water*.

Lafcadio Hearn's *The Reconciliation*, retold in the *Kwaidan* film as *Black Hair*, is

prime example of japanese ghostly psychological horror built around a central motif of long black hair.

The story tells that a young samurai found himself in poverty when the master he served fell into ruin. Desperately wishing to advance his station in life, he found an appointment outside the capital and divorced his lovely wife, believing that he could find another woman with higher social standing to marry instead. He quickly found a new wife who fit the bill and moved with her to a distant province.

But the samurai soon came to regret his choice for his new wife was cruel and selfish, and their marriage unhappy. He quickly realized that he still loved his first wife, and every day he was haunted by the choice he had made and the hurt he had caused her. With every waking moment he thought of her long glossy black hair, the feel and the scent of it. Secretly, he resolved to one day return to her and make things right.

Eventually, he was freed from his term, and at once he hurried back to Kyoto to seek out his former wife. However, when he returned in the dead of night to the house they once shared, it looked deserted, with tall weeds growing. He knocked at the sliding door, but no one answered. Finding the door open, he entered; the house that awaited him was cold and empty, the rooms dark.

He went further into the house until he reached his ex-wife's chambers and was delighted to find a glow of light. There she was, sewing by lamplight, as young and as fair as she had ever been, her hair soft and luxurious. At once, he took her in his arms and buried his face in her silky locks, telling her of his love for her and his regret at his actions. His sweet gentle wife forgave him at once.

They talked late into the night, telling one another of all that had happened in the time they'd spent apart, although the wife spoke little of her own circumstances. Eventually, as dawn was breaking, the samurai fell asleep.

He awoke later in the morning to bright sunlight, but was shocked to find himself lying on bare, dusty boards. Had it all been a dream? But no, his wife was there beside him! He leaned over to look upon her... and screamed. All that remained of his

LEFT: **Michiyo Aratama (1930–2001) plays a wife in *The Black Hair,* one part of the anthology movie *Kwaidan*.**

beautiful wife was a corpse, so rotted and wasted that she was barely more than bones – bones and long, tangled black hair.

Composing himself, he went out to ask someone from the neighbourhood about the house. He came across a local who told him, 'No one lives there now. It used to belong to the wife of a samurai; he divorced her to marry another woman and moved away, leaving her behind. The stress made her sick, and with no relatives to help care for her, she died alone and destitute.'

Haunted dolls

Haunted dolls are a staple of urban legends in many cultures, and Japan is no exception. There is a supposedly haunted doll on display at Mannenji Temple in Hokkaido. Various stories

Traditional Japanese dolls at Awashima Shrine in Wakayama Prefecture.

surround it, but the version the temple tells is that in 1918, a family bought their three-year old daughter Kikuko an *okappa-ningyo*, a traditional Japanese doll with a bob haircut and dressed in a kimono. Kikuko loved the doll and took her everywhere with her, naming her Okiku. However, a few months later, the young girl caught an infection and died suddenly. Due to circumstances at the time, the family were unable to lay the doll to rest with Kikuko, and they placed it on their household altar along with their daughter's ashes. However, one day the family noticed that the doll's hair was growing longer; it was no longer set in a neat little bob, but had grown wild down past its shoulders. They became convinced that Kikuko's spirit had taken up residence within the doll.

When the family had to move, they felt it best that the doll should stay near Kikuko's grave, and so they entrusted it to the local temple. It has remained there since, receiving occasional haircuts as its hair continues to grow, and is on display for anyone who feels brave enough to look upon its haunted countenance.

Seven Mysteries

Local unexplained phenomena would often be grouped together and referred to as the seven mysteries of the area. Famous examples include the Seven Mysteries of Suwa Grand Shrine and the Enshuu Seven Mysteries, although there are also countless local examples, most of which were only passed on orally. Today, the seven mysteries format is mostly used for urban legends, particularly school-based ones.

The 'seven mysteries of a school' is a well-worn trope in anime and manga; usually, the first six mysteries will have a banal explanation, reminiscent of the cartoon franchise *Scooby-Doo*, whereas the final mystery will either be real or left ambiguous.

Often mentioned in the same breath as the 'spooky seven mysteries' is the 'test of courage', called *kimodameshi* in Japanese, a game in which the participants dare one another to visit creepy places such as a cemetery, dark forest or haunted area of a school. It is often played during the summer months on school trips. Unlike the dares typically undertaken by teens in the UK or

BELOW: **Suwa Grand Shrine in Nagano Prefecture has its own Seven Mysteries.**

USA, the participants are not sent off alone, but rather go as a group and try to encourage one another to hold their nerves.

Aka Manto

Legends of this toilet spirit date back to the 1930s. *Aka Manto*, which literally means 'red cape', is a male spirit who haunts female public or school toilets. He is dressed in a flowing red cape and hides his face behind a mask. He appears when a person is sitting on the toilet and asks if they want red or blue toilet paper; if they choose 'red', the victim will be lacerated to death, leaving their corpse drenched in their blood. Answering 'blue' will also result in death, usually via strangulation or exsanguination. The only way to survive is to either ignore the spirit or answer that you do not want either kind.

The legend also spread to Korea when the peninsula was under Japanese rule between 1910 and 1945. The 2021 hit South Korean television show *Squid Game* references the legend when the protagonist is offered a choice between a red or a blue tile by the character recruiting them for the titular game. Creator Hwang Dong-hyuk explained that, in the same way that Aka Manto will kill you no matter what choice you make, whichever tile the character in the show picks, they are more than likely going to become a contestant and lose their life.

Hanako-san of the Toilet

Another popular toilet-related urban legend among schoolchildren is that of Hanako-san, the spirit of a young girl who haunts school toilets. How she came to haunt the toilets varies wildly; in some versions of the legend, she was killed while playing hide-and-seek during a WWII air raid, while in others she killed herself in the school toilet due to bullying.

Children often dare one another to summon Hanako-san by going into the girls' toilets, knocking three times on the third stall, and asking if Hanako-san is there. If she is, then she will answer 'Yes, I am' and a bloody, ghostly hand will appear which may or may not pull the individual into the toilet and down to hell.

The origins of Hanako-san are murky, but her appearance in manga, films and games has entrenched her place in popular culture and modern folklore. The manga series *Toilet-bound Hanako-kun* by AidaIro that began serialization in 2014 reimagines the ghost of Hanako-san as a young boy. Perhaps this interpretation will eventually become part of the established canon surrounding Hanako-san.

Kuchisake-onna

Probably the best-known figure from Japanese urban legend, the 'slit-mouthed woman' has been referred to as both an *onryō* and a modern-day *yōkai*. Kuchisake-onna is the vengeful spirit of a woman who was mutilated by having the corners of her mouth slit from ear to ear. The origins of these injuries differ depending on the version of the tale being told; she may have been the wife of a samurai who was punished for her adultery; she have been attacked by another woman who was jealous of her beauty, or she may have been the victim of a botched medical procedure. Either way, she has returned to the land of the living, and she seeks victims of her own.

She has long, straight black hair and pale skin, and she carries a sharp instrument such as a surgical knife or a long pair of scissors. Her face is partially obscured by a surgical mask or even a hand-held fan.

ABOVE: The urban legend about Hanako-san of the Toilet was the inspiration for a 1995 Japanese horror film.

There is a pattern that an encounter with Kuchisake-onna follows. First, she will ask 'Am I beautiful?' If the person answers in the negative, Kuchisake-onna will kill them with her weapon. If they answer in the affirmative, she will reveal her mutilated mouth. Then, she repeats her question: 'Am I beautiful?' If the person now answers 'no' or shows fright or disgust, they will be killed. If they respond with 'yes', then Kuchisake-onna will slice the person's own mouth at the corners to mirror her own disfigurement.

There are apparently a few ways to survive an encounter with this particular spirit. One is to answer her questions by saying that she looks 'average', which will distract her and give the victim time to run away. Another is to throw *bekko ame*, a kind of boiled sweet at her, which she will then stop to pick up. Yet another recommends saying 'pomade' six times to banish her.

Kuchisake-onna has her roots in the Edo period. Shungyosai Hayami's illustrated book *Ehon Sayoshigure* (1801) tells a brief story about a patron visiting a brothel in the famous Yoshiwara red-light district of the capital. While there, he called out to a courtesan walking down the corridor ahead of him, wishing to engage her in flirtatious banter. When the woman turned around, he found her to be horribly disfigured, her mouth sliced open from ear to ear. The patron fainted from fright and never visited the brothel again.

The modern resurgence of Kuchisake-onna originated in Gifu Prefecture at the end of 1978, and by January 1979 reports quickly spread in newspapers and on local radio shows. The mass media coverage led to terror and panic among young students and their parents, although it quickly subsided once schools broke up for summer. In the same year, it became popular in hostess clubs in Ginza for the hostess to cover her mouth and ask 'Am I pretty?' The client had to respond with 'pomade' or 'sweets'. Shigeru Mizuki strengthened Kuchisake-onna's contemporary popularity when he included her in a *yōkai* encyclopedia in 1984.

In the 1990s, with the boom in plastic surgery, Kuchisake-onna became associated with botched procedures. The internet has further popularized her story, and she is a frequent subject of fan art, both beautiful and horrific.

OPPOSITE: Translated as *The Slit-Mouthed Woman* in English, Kuchisake-onna is a terrifying woman with a mouth sliced at the corners. Poster from a 2007 film inspired by the urban legend.

ABOVE: **Enryō Inoue was a prominent scholar during the Meiji period colloquially known as 'Professor Spectre' due to his interest in supernatural phenomenon and debunking superstitions.**

Kokkuri

This game gained popularity during the Meiji period (1868–1912) and was based on the Western Victorian séance in which people attempted to communicate with spirits. The spirit that is summoned through the *kokkuri* ritual is called *kokkuri-san*.

Today, *kokkuri* is something closer to a Ouija board. A *torii* symbol is drawn at the top of a sheet of paper with 'yes' and 'no' written on each side and a letter grid beneath it. A coin is used as a planchette. The door or a window to the room must be left open when playing for the spirit to enter and closed after it leaves, and within 24 hours of playing the game, the paper should be burned and the coin spent. First popular with girls during the 1970s, it is still played today.

As with the Ouija board in the West, modern scientific studies have investigated *kokkuri* and concluded that it is an example of the power of superstition on the subconscious mind. One such investigator was the prolific philosopher, Inoue Enryō. He pioneered something he called 'mystery studies' whereby he categorized native folk beliefs and superstitions and offered rational explanations for them, in essence 'debunking' them, which led to his nickname Doctor Spectre.

Curse of the Colonel

Perhaps one of the most bizarre urban legends is that the Hanshin Tigers baseball team is cursed by the ghost of KFC founder and mascot Colonel Sanders. In 1985, the Kansai-based Hanshin Tigers, considered the underdogs of Japanese top-level professional baseball, surprised the nation when they won the Japan Series for the first (and so far last) time.

Fans gathered at Ebisu Bridge in Dōtonbori, Osaka to celebrate. They chanted the players' names and with each name a fan who resembled the player jumped off the bridge into the canal. However, when they got to MVP Randy Bass, there was no Caucasian person to represent him; instead, the crowd grabbed a plastic statue of Colonel Sanders from outside a nearby KFC restaurant to use as an effigy, and into the water it went. This supposedly kicked off the curse, and the Hanshin Tigers were doomed to an 18-year losing streak. There were many unsuccessful attempts to retrieve the statue during this time that often featured in TV shows. When, in 2003, the Tigers won the Central League, thousands of fans jumped into the river, and one tragically drowned during the chaotic revelry. The Tigers lost the Japan Series and the curse continued.

On 10 March 2009, the statue was finally recovered.

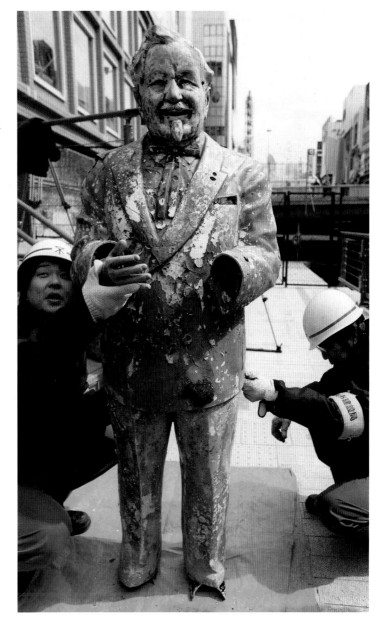

BELOW: **A statue of Colonel Sanders that was thrown into a river in Osaka in 1985 is said to be behind the Hanshin Tiger's losing streak. It was finally found and pulled out of the river in 2009.**

Unfortunately, the Colonel is still missing his left hand and his glasses, and it is said that the curse will not be lifted until they are reunited. As the original restaurant is no longer there, the recovered statue now stands in the branch near the Koshien baseball stadium.

Inokashira Park curse

This modern urban legend relates to the ancient goddess mentioned in an earlier chapter – Benzaiten. There are many romantic spots in Japan that are rumoured to bring luck to visiting couples; for example, it is said that a couple who kiss on the Yokohama Cosmo Clock 21 Ferris Wheel will stay together. However, just as there are lucky spots, there are also cursed ones. Supposedly, any couple that take one of the iconic swan paddle boats out into lake in the middle of Inokashira Park are doomed to break up due to Benzaiten's jealousy.

BELOW: **The lake in Inokashira Park in Tokyo is supposedly cursed, and the park has also been the site of a gruesome crime.**

Inokashira Park itself has a gruesome past. On 23 April 1994, parts of a dismembered body were found in a bin in the park; the head, chest and genitals were missing and have never been found. The cause of death could not be determined, but the body had been drained of its blood and carefully cut using an electric saw, suggesting that the perpetrator had medical training. Although the victim was identified, the case remains unsolved to this day, giving people another reason to feel spooked when visiting the park.

Jinmenken

The *jinmenken* is a human-faced dog that appears in urban areas under cover of darkness. They can run as fast as 100km/h (62mph) and will race along beside cars in the dead of night. If a car overtakes them, it will end up in an accident. They can also be found rooting through bins, and when shouted at to go away, they will turn back with their human face and say 'leave me alone'. The *jinmenken* is said to be either the result of genetic experimentation, or the ghost of a person who was hit by a car while walking their dog.

The concept of *jinmenken* dates back to the early 19th century, but the modern version spread, as many urban legends do, among schoolchildren in 1989 before being reported in the mass media. Since then, they have featured in the role-playing video game franchise *Yo-kai Watch*, and with their newfound popularity may well soon be included in the established *yōkai* canon.

Japanese 'Creepypasta'

The invention and proliferation of the internet has provided another avenue for urban legends to spread, this time at lightning speed. The English term 'creepypasta' refers to short horror stories posted on the internet that are intended to scare the reader. Like the earlier *kaidan*, many of these stories purport to be true; some use the instant communication facilitated by the internet to be told in real time, as though the writer is experiencing the phenomenon as they type. It becomes a kind of interactive fiction as the poster asks other message board users for advice, adding to the realism. The best-known

THE CAUSE OF DEATH COULD NOT BE DETERMINED, BUT THE BODY HAD BEEN DRAINED OF ITS BLOOD AND CAREFULLY CUT USING AN ELECTRIC SAW, SUGGESTING THAT THE PERPETRATOR HAD MEDICAL TRAINING.

English-language creepypasta is the infamous Slender Man, but other spine-tingling stories originated on Japanese message boards and forums.

Red Room Curse

One of the earliest Japanese urban legends on the internet began in the late 1990s and warns of a red pop-up ad that foretells the user's death. The origins have been traced back to an Adobe Flash horror animation. It was said that while browsing the internet, an unlucky user might suddenly be presented with a red pop-up box on which black text asked the reader: 'Do you like xxx?', with 'xxx' being any random thing. When the person tries to close the box, it reappears, this time with text asking: 'Do you like the Red Room?' Then, the whole screen turns red and displays a list of the Red Room's previous victims. The current victim will then sense a presence behind them before losing consciousness. They will later be discovered dead with the walls of the room painted red with their blood.

Like many urban legends, the Red Room Curse preyed on existing fears; the internet was new and not well understood, and the curse seemed believable. The legend gained further notoriety in 2004 after the Sasebo slashing, in which an 11-year-old schoolgirl killed her 12-year-old classmate during lunch break at their elementary school in Sasebo, Nagasaki Prefecture, by slitting her throat with a box cutter. Media reported that the perpetrator was a fan of the original Red Room flash animation, which only added fuel to the urban legend's fire. Like similar incidents around the world, the case was used to stoke fears over the effects of internet usage on children as well as concerns about violent media, as the girl was also said to be a fan of the 2000 movie *Battle Royale* in which a group of high-school students are forced to fight to the death by a totalitarian government.

Kunekune

Meaning 'wriggling body', *kunekune* is an example of what could be termed an internet-derived *yōkai*. It first appeared in 2001 in the form of a short horror story on the bulletin board 2channel, which inspired others to post their own 'eyewitness' accounts.

OPPOSITE: **Onoe Matsusuke as the Ghost of the Murdered Wife Oiwa, in** *A Tale of Horror from the Yotsuya Station on the Tokaido Road,* **by Utagawa Toyokuni I (1812).**

ABOVE: **Several shocking incidents in which young students murdered classmates caused a panic about the kinds of stories children were being exposed to on the internet.**

Like other creepypasta, accounts are written in the first person singular, taking the form of a reported encounter.

The *kunekune* is slender, white and humanoid, its body seemingly made of paper or fabric. It appears in rice fields on hot summer days and wriggles its limbs as though buffeted by gusts of wind even when there is none. It is only visible at a distance; those close to it, such as farmers working the fields, are seemingly unaware of its presence. It is said that if someone attempts to look at a *kunekune* up close, they will go insane. Other lore states that if you get too close to one it will kill you, but so long as you keep your distance, it will ignore you.

While it seems that the first *kunekune* stories were clearly presented as fictional, this soon evolved into a mix of faux-reports as well as people's genuine accounts of strange sightings they believed could be attributed to the *kunekune*. As we have seen in the previous section, textile-based *yōkai* such as *ittan-momen* already existed within Japanese folklore, and *kunekune* may be an evolution of these. Explanations for supposed sightings of *kunekune* are that people have mistaken a scarecrow or a wick drain for something more sinister, or that heat haze or dehydration are playing tricks on their eyes.

Kisaragi Station

Like other urban legends, Kisaragi Station comes from the internet bulletin board 2channel. The story was posted in real-time in early 2004 on a thread of the site's occult board dedicated to recounting 'true' strange and supernatural experiences.

While message boards such as 2channel are fairly niche, they were, and still are, often the starting point for internet memes that subsequently become widespread across the internet. In 2014, Kisaragi Station made the jump to Twitter, leading to mainstream interest, and it has since featured in many manga, anime, games and other media. A film simply called *Kisaragi Station* starring Yuri Tsunematsu was released in 2022. The legend is also popular in Taiwan and China, and as an English-language creepypasta.

A user named Hasumi posted to the thread that she had just woken up after nodding off during her usual commute to work to find all the other passengers in the train carriage asleep. The train was speeding along without stopping, and Hasumi couldn't contact the conductor or driver. She conversed with users on the

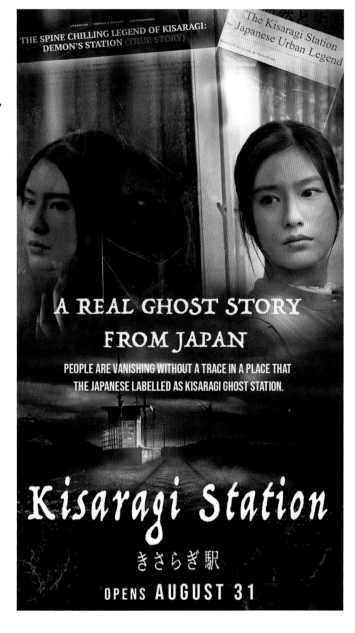

BELOW: A movie based on the Kisaragi Station creepypasta was released in 2022.

message board about her confusion and interacted with them as they offered advice.

At last, after about an hour, the train stopped at Kisaragi Station. It was late at night, and the place was deserted. Message board users alerted her to the fact that there was no record of such a station existing. Hasumi disembarked from the train and tried to find a taxi or someone to help her, but there was no one around. Eventually, she found a phone box and called her parents, but they had no idea how to find her and advised her to call the police; but when she did so, she was written off as a prankster.

Users then suggested she wait for the first train of the day, but the situation was becoming more menacing. Hasumi reported hearing drumbeats and the sound of a bell in the distance, as

BELOW: **Ishinomaki is one of several cities that were devastated by the Tōhoku earthquake and resulting tsunami on March 11, 2011.**

though some otherworldly festival were taking place. Terrified to turn around and go back to the station, Hasumi continued along the tracks. Suddenly, she heard someone yell: 'Hey! Don't walk on the tracks, it's dangerous!' Turning around, she saw a one-legged old man who immediately vanished.

In a state of fear, she continued, falling and hurting herself several times in the process, until she came to a tunnel; screwing up her courage, she decided to venture inside. When she reached the end of the tunnel, she encountered a friendly man who offered her a ride. With no other choice, she accepted. The man summoned a train, which she boarded against the other users' advice.

As she sat aboard the train, she realized that it was heading deeper and deeper into the mountains, where no train should go. The man was now completely silent, and Hasumi felt that something was deeply wrong.

Her last message said: 'My battery's almost dead. This whole situation is weird, so I'm going to try to get away. He's started muttering weird things to himself. I'm going to prepare for the worst, so this will be my last post for now.' Hasumi was never heard from again.

AT LAST… THE TRAIN STOPPED AS KISARAGI STATION. IT WAS LATE AT NIGHT, AND THE PLACE WAS DESERTED. MESSAGE BOARD USERS ALERTED HER TO THE FACT THAT THERE WAS NO RECORD OF SUCH A STATION EXISTING.

Ghost Passengers

Like trains, cars also feature in urban legends. One phenomenon is that of 'ghost passengers' reported by taxi drivers; they stop to pick up a fare, only to find that the person vanishes into thin air during the ride.

In 2016, student researcher Yuka Kudo wrote a thesis in which she interviewed people in Ishinomaki, Miyagi Prefecture, where 3500 people died when a tsunami triggered by a 9.0 magnitude earthquake swept through the city's streets. One of the most haunting stories is told from the perspective of a 53-year-old taxi driver from the area:

'It was probably about three months after the disaster. I could tell you exactly if I looked at my ledger, but it was the beginning of summer. One night I was waiting for a fare around Ishinomaki Station when a woman got in. She was dressed in a puffer coat as if it was the middle of winter.'

RIGHT: A man lights candles during a lantern ceremony to mark the 10th anniversary of the Tōhoku natural disaster.

RIGHT: A man lights candles during a lantern ceremony to mark the 10th anniversary of the Tōhoku natural disaster.

She looked around 30 years old. When he asked her destination, she replied with 'Minamihama'. *'I thought that was strange. I asked her 'Are you sure? There's basically nothing left there. Why are you going there? Are you not hot in that coat?'* The woman responded in a trembling voice with her own question: *'Am I dead?'*

Startled, the driver looked into the mirror to find the back seat empty.

At first he was too terrified to even move, but thinking back on it now, he says, *'I suppose it's not that strange. So many people died in the disaster – some of them must have unfinished business. I'm sure it was a ghost that I saw. I'm not scared anymore. If I saw another customer dressed in winter garb waiting for a ride, I'd pick them up and treat them like any other passenger.'*

Kudo's findings were published in a book along with other investigations into supernatural phenomena that have been reported across the affected areas. It has been suggested by some sociologists that these experiences result from a form of shared post-traumatic stress disorder and collective grief. Nearly 20,000 people lost their lives in the 2011 Tōhoku earthquake and tsunami with many victims still unaccounted for, and the devastation, which was witnessed in real-time on television and internet broadcasts, undoubtedly struck a psychological blow to the entire nation. These encounters serve as a reminder of the intrinsic connection between ghosts and human psychology.

Japan has a long and rich tradition of myth and legend, from the creation myths in the country's earliest written works and orally transmitted folklore to modern-day urban legends and 'netlore' that similarly blurs the lines between fact and fiction.

Myths and legends are concepts that take root in the collective consciousness where they evolve along with the changing exterior world, both reflecting and shaping a national psyche. To better understand a culture, we can look to the stories people tell to and about themselves and the world around them. In doing so, we can discover aspects that are both unique and universal to cultures everywhere – all while enjoying a rich and vibrant legacy of art and storytelling.

BELOW: **The Bon Festival is held in August at the height of summer and honours the spirits of one's ancestors.**

BIBLIOGRAPHY

Ashkenazi, M. (2003). *Handbook of Japanese Mythology.* Oxford University Press.

Aston, W. G. (1972). *Nihongi: Chronicles of Japan from the Earliest Times to A.D. 697.* Tuttle Publishing. (Original work published 1956.).

Foster, M. D. (2015). *The Book of Yōkai.* University of California Press.

Frydman, J. (2022). *The Japanese Myths.* Thames & Hudson.

Isomae, J., & Araki, H. (2022). *Japanese Myths & Legends.* Flame Tree Publishing.

Keene, D. (1964). *The Manyōshū : the Nippon Gakujutsu Shinkōkai Translation of One Thousand Poems.* Columbia University Press.

Kimbrough, K., & Shirane, H. (Eds.). (2018). *Monsters, Animals, and Other Worlds: A Collection of Short Medieval Japanese Tales.* Columbia University Press.

Leeming, D. (2005). *The Oxford Companion to World Mythology.* Oxford University Press.

McMillan, P. (2018). *One Hundred Poets, One Poem Each: A Treasury of Classical Japanese Verse.* St. Ives: Penguin Classics.

Mitford, A. B., & Foster, M. D. (2019). *Japanese Legends and Folklore.* Tuttle Publishing.

Murasaki, S. (1925). *The Tale of Genji.* (A. Waley, Trans.) Boston and New York: The Riverside Press Cambridge. (Original work published n.d.).

Nakamura, K. (1973). *Miraculous Stories from the Japanese Buddhist Tradition: The Nihon Ryōiki of the Monk Kyōkai.* Cambridge, MA: Harvard University Press.

Yasumaro, Ō. (1919). *The Kojiki: Records of Ancient Matters.* (B. H. Chamberlain, Trans.) (Original work published n.d.).

Yasumaro, Ō. (2014). *The Kojiki.* (G. Heldt, Trans.) Columbia University Press. (Original work published n.d.).

INDEX

Picture credits